THE PIT

THE PIT

Enrico Bernard

THE PIT

An Italian Paradox

A Novel and A Play

Translation by Marco Remo Zanelli

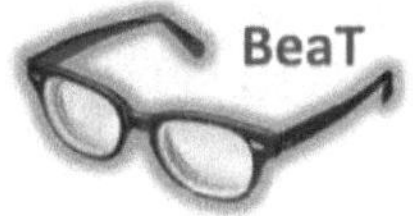

THE PIT

AUTOBIOGRAPHICAL LAMENT OF WORKING MAN, ORESTE CIRIOLA (PROFESSIONAL SLACKER), ALSO KNOWN BY HIS FRIENDS AS "ORI," WHOSE BALLS HAVE LITERALLY BEEN BUSTED BY EVERYONE AND ABOUT EVERYTHING THAT HE IS SLOWLY REALIZING WORK IS TIRING, AND IT WOULD BE BETTER... MUCH, MUCH BETTER, TO CALL IN SICK – PREFERABLY FOREVER.

CHAPTER ONE

Jump To It!

The Boss has been closely watching Ori for a while. He's being a wise ass, he thinks, or else he's just an idiot. *Why is he working so hard? Who asked him to work so hard that the shovel would create calluses on his hands?* The Boss ordered Ori to dig a hole, that's all, but that dimwit has burrowed a fucking endless pit.

"Damn, what a hole! It reminds me of your sister's… never mind!" the Boss mumbles to Ori, biting his lip.

Actually, the Boss is not completely wrong. First, Ori broke through the asphalt with a pneumatic hammer, then he started wielding a pick – better than King Arthur wielding his sword during the Crusades – and finally, he started shoveling out mounds of dirt until he disappeared into the pit altogether. *This is insane, who the hell asked him to do that, where on God's earth does he want go?* is the Boss's Hamletic query.

The Boss suspects that the union heads have coerced or incited him, but he doesn't know to what end. Usually, they make slackers like Ori do as little work as possible, not much more than the minimum necessary. Maybe they want an excuse to assert his worker rights, or rack up backpay, so he's certainly someone to keep an eye on. If Pit Management didn't expressly ask him to work so hard, why in the world would he sweat through seven different shirts.

"Management… Ha!" Ori complains under his breath while continuing to dig. *There isn't any damn Pit Management,* he thinks, *considering nothing at all is being managed here. They give you a shovel and tell you to dig, and you dig, and no one tells to you to stop. So, you continue. You continue on and try to do your job to the best of your ability. That way, no one can reprimand or criticize you, and at the same time, you prevent them from accusing the rest of the working class of being a mass of fucking slackers.*

Ori's shovel hits a hard an impenetrable layer of ground. He then takes the pick and swings it once, twice, three times, with enough force to break through the cement walls of a bunker, but the dirt doesn't move. He even has trouble just grazing the surface. The pick only causes a distant echo that reverberates like underground thunder (or like farting under a blanket – Ori smiles at the thought of one of his renown, though feared intestinal gas eruptions).

What if I've reached that layer of iron that separates us from the planet's entire mass of smoldering shit? is Ori's thinking, pondering the thought for a moment, though basing his theory on insufficient geological knowledge acquired from watching quiz shows, which are the only passion in his neither happy nor unhappy, but simply passive and empty existence as a TV spectator. *No, I couldn't have dug that far,* he immediately reassures himself. *And, if I had, I wouldn't be standing here talking about it, because had I reached the doors of Hell, the lava would have fried my balls like two eggs, sunney side up.* Note the difficulty an illiterate like Ori has in just thinking the word *sunny.*

It's true that Ori constantly thinks of his bread and butter, but more in the literal sense; food gives him a sense of existence and of passing time. For him, the progression of daily events is only a means to the next meal: breakfast is a prelude to a mid-morning goodie, which precedes lunch, then is followed by a snack, after which it's time for dinner and the evening ritual of ending up on the sofa with a nightcap in hand, watching some rubbish on TV.

He's unsettled at the fact that the shovel, pick and pneumatic hammer are unable to penetrate any further. *My wife was probably right,* he thinks, *when she said I've become too flaccid… and I'm unable to bore the way I use to when the drill tip was made of stainless steel and the handle was as hard as that of a broom stick! Now I'm going to have to skip lunch because of the setback, dammit!* So, not knowing how to cover his ass, Ori lets out a shout of frustration in a desperate attempt to pass the problem (and the shovel) off to the right personnel.

"Hey, Boss! I've hit something hard! Hey, we've hit bottom! Did you hear me? We've accidentally hit bottom… the bottom, dammit! It's never happened before… but it had to happen to me! What a terrible day… or rather, what a shitty day! No one gives a damn about anything…"

Once the Boss, having left for a moment to take care of a bodily need, hears Ori's shouts, he's forced to tense up his prostate, re-sheathe his dripping penis and pull up his zipper, catching the skin of his scrotum. After letting out a deafening scream of pain, he rushes to the edge of the pit where he sees a desolate and mortified bonehead, Ori, popping out of the hole like a cuckoo emerging from an unwound clock.

"It's happened, Boss."

The Boss is completely dumbfounded. "Dammit, Ori! What's happened?

Ori doesn't know how to communicate the disaster to his immediate superior. He'd like to explain it in an indirect and roundabout way, but the technical terms escape him, because he's not scholastically adept at metaphors and circumlocution. So, he's forced to lower his head and be candid, "We've accidentally hit bottom."

"Dammit, Ori!" the Boss echoes himself.

"Don't' be upset with me, Boss."

"No? Who should I be upset with, in your opinion?"

"Well, it's the pit that caused us to hit bottom…"

"So, it's the pit's fault that *you* hit its bottom? Are you pulling my chain, you bastard?"

Ori doesn't know how to get out of the bad situation and would just like to sink back into the ditch. He has only enough energy to admit, "I only wanted to tell you that we've hit bottom, Boss, that's all."

With his eyes busting out of their sockets, and his balls too, considering Ori has busted them pretty badly, the Boss closely scrutinizes the worker.

"You know, I've been watching you for some time now, and I don't like you, Ori. No, I don't like you at all."

At this point, a thought comes to mind, and Ori suggests, "Take a look, Boss, and you'll see what a disaster we have on our hands."

The Boss sticks his neck out to look into the pit, but he's not able to see anything at bottom of crater, not even if there is a veritable bottom. So, he bluffs and says, "Yeah, I see it… son of a bitch! Nice situation we have here. Are you sure you've really hit bottom?"

"Damn! It's hard as rock, listen… hey guys, let the Boss hear the sound of the bottom."

A raspberry sound is emitted from the pit.

"Did you hear that, Boss? What do you think?" Ori asks dumbfounded.

The Boss is also speechless. "It really does seem to be the bottom. But I'm not surprised… I mean, no more than usual. Dig, dig, dig, and we were bound to hit it, sooner or later, right?"

"But that's what we're here for!" Ori tries to reassure the Boss.

The Boss is baffled. He hesitates and continues to shake his head, not knowing what to do or which saint to address, if it were to come to that. "We can't go any further, right?"

"Right. There's nowhere else to go. And when you hit bottom, it's nothing to celebrate. Now it's even going to be tough to climb back out, to boot."

"At least we can't fall any lower," the Boss consoles himself.

"As long as there's not a second bottom," Ori counters, immediately regretting putting the Boss's convictions in doubt – uncertain convictions that are open ended, just like the concept of a bottomless pit. However, despite the pit's uncertainties, at least there was still something to believe in, which would have been better than nothing at all at the moment.

The Boss understands that Ori is thinking and talking off the top of his fucking head, just to say anything, so he cuts him short, "A second bottom? Bullshit."

"If you say so!"

"Do you see anything of value down there, rather?"

"It's pitch dark, Boss."

"Are you sure there are no cracks of light?"

"We would have noticed them. We wouldn't have missed a crack of light in the pit, no matter how small."

"And if you had found one, you would've sealed it up immediately, right Ori?"

"Right, Boss. We would have absolutely closed it up. There are no cracks, I swear."

"Remember, there can be no cracks."

Ori comically jumps to attention placing the shovel handle in front of him, like a standard issue army rifle he doesn't know how to use. "Yes, sir, Boss!"

The Boss nods, pleased to see Ori has gone back to being the dutiful little soldier that he is.

"Good, that's how I like you, obedient and disciplined."

Ori stays at attention for a few moments, then deflates like a badly made souffle. "Other orders, Boss?"

There's an embarrassing silence from the Boss, who doesn't immediately understand the existential and metaphysical implications of Ori's question, so he fumbles his words and says, "Don't know, should I have more?"

"I would think so. A respected Boss always has orders to give. So, what should I do?"

"Your job, for fuck's sake, which is to obey without making a big deal of things…"

"Obey what?" Ori asks for the record, his work record that is, though he knows it would be better to keep quiet to avoid triggering useless and counterproductive arguments.

"Just follow orders, you imbecile!" the Boss explodes in anger.

"What orders? There haven't been any for some time now!"

"The order, for the moment, is to maintain order. Then we'll see. As the proverbs goes: 'everything in due time.' Or should I think you're in a hurry to change the order of things… the social order, you dirty traitor?"

Ori – or Oreste Ciriola, as the name appears on his birth certificate – doesn't give a damn if he's considered a subversive or anything else. He belongs to the Party of Bread and Butter, just as his name, a type of Roman loaf, alludes to. He would do anything to earn a living and get ahead – if he were any good at it, he would even prostitute himself, just like the union does, he thinks… with all due respect, of course.

"If it were me, you know where I would have told the orders to go, Boss? To he…"

"Quiet!"

"Can't I even curse?"

"Why? Can you even tell me what you're complaining about?"

"A little bit about everything, Boss."

"You think complaining is a good thing?"

"No, Boss, certainly not."

"You see, I'm right."

"You're always right, Boss. But…" Ori scratches his head. A scattering of dust and dirt falls from the thinning hair adhered to his scalp with brilliantine. He's wearing beat-up shoes, and there's a rip in his work overalls right in the middle of his buttocks, like it's been torn open by one of those intestinal gas eruptions Ori had thought of earlier.

The Boss looks him up and down. "What now, Ori?"

Ori stops scratching his noggin. He's baffled as to how someone is unable to grasp the situation. It's extremely clear to him! Is it possible the proof is not immediately evident to the Boss, who theoretically, should know more than him when it comes to pits, for the simple fact that it is he who is supervising the dig? So, he tries to explain in his own words by asserting, "When you hit bottom, you start asking yourself: What do we do now, just sit here and twiddle our thumbs? Orders aren't coming down from above, and no one knows what to do... so, the question becomes: What if they never get here? How long can we sit around doing nothing?"

"Enough! No *ifs*, *ands* or *buts*. All we need now are more of your hair-brained doubts. The orders *will* get here. I can't assure you they'll come on time, but they'll get here. You can bet your ass on it!"

"Only if you bet yours, too, Boss!"

"You're skeptical, Ori?"

"If it were any other time, I could've gotten by without other orders. When there was still a lot to dig, for example, the only order that came down was to 'Dig, dig, dig.' Now that we've hit bottom, though, and we don't know if there will more to dig tomorrow, we need immediate orders, some certainty about our future, otherwise we are left at the mercy of only rumors that are unclear. Does this seem right to you?"

"You could've have obeyed when there was still more to dig, and orders to follow. Now that there are none, you want something to carry out. But it's too late."

Ori doesn't come to the same conclusion, though he did brood about it for long periods of time in the darkness of the pit, when the Boss was nowhere to be found down there, and there was still digging to do amongst the sewer sludge and mice.

"So, if there are no other orders, I can even do without a Boss, how about that!"

"Do without me? Have you lost your mind? You damn well need me here, there's no doubt about that!"

"No, I don't," objects Ori, who has now set sail on a corporate collision course.

"Hey, hey! Be careful. Consider this a warning…"

Ori doesn't hold back and bursts forward like a river overflowing its banks. "There's no need for a boss when that boss has no more orders to give. Fact is, if you don't have orders to give, and nothing for me to obey, you are no longer my Boss. You're nothing, not even a good friend, an acquaintance nor… I don't know… my wife's lover! Nothing. Get it, Boss? You're absolutely nothing, nil, nada, zippo, zilch. A complete zero!"

The Boss looks at him with an air of commiseration, deciding on how to proceed and what disciplinary actions to take. However, the insolent look on Ori's face facilitates the otherwise distressing task of pronouncing his verdict: "You're fired, then – if that's the way you feel."

"Oh, that's great! For what?"

"For insubordination."

"What does that word mean?"

"It means you are refusing to follow orders, you idiot!"

"No, it's *you* who are refusing to give them."

Here we go again, the Boss is thinking, angrily biting his already mangled lip, on which he takes out his ill-concealed nervousness. *Ori wants to make things difficult for me right front of everyone in the work zone. I have to remain calm and cold blooded to be able to answer in kind. I hate being put on the spot – especially by an underling!*

The Boss clicks his heals in a military and uncontestable manner. "The order is to not follow any orders, seeing as there are none. How's that? Happy now, you chicken legged bigshot?"

Ori, however, doesn't ignore the rude remark, and he continues to react to the insults and abuse by provoking his superior, "Oh, no! That answer is just a little too convenient for someone in the position of a boss."

"And obeying orders only when you feel like it is just a little too convenient for someone in the position of a worker. It's not fair, Ori, to demand things at the precise moment society doesn't have the luxury of being at your service to satisfy your every whim and clean up your every mess."

"Well," Ori smugly shoots back, "is there at least someone higher up who's able to send down more orders?"

The Boss tries to stay calm. "I hope so, by God! Now that you, I mean, *we* – considering we're in the same boat – have hit bottom, I, too, am awaiting orders, in a certain sense. And have no doubt about it, the situation is equally as embarrassing for me."

"Maybe," Ori interjects and sighs. He reaches into the pit and grabs his lunchbox. Then, from under a mound of dirt he pulls out a bottle of white wine, which he buried earlier to keep cool and out of the scorching sun. He sits and gets ready to eat.

The Boss is dumbfounded and snaps, "Oh, wonderful, great, good for you! Right in the middle of a tough situation, you only worried about filling your stomach!"

"But I always think better on a full stomach," Ori says. Without waiting for the Boss to prepare a counter-attack and catch Ori off guard, he fires a howitzer of a query: "Do you believe in the orders, Boss?"

"The questions you ask are fucking stupid, Ori!"

"Well, maybe we weren't supposed to hit bottom. Maybe we were supposed to stop sooner. At least that's what I think… so there."

"Did someone force a shovel in your hand and then say: 'go ahead and hit bottom?'"

"No," Ori admits, enjoying the sight of the four-layered sandwich.

"What were your orders?" the Boss interrogates Ori, while also eyeing his sandwich.

"Dig, dig, dig."

"And did you dig?"

"Absolutely! Feel these calluses! When I grab my pecker to shake it off after taking a piss, it feels like I'm putting it between two sheets of sand paper."

"See? Either out of incompetence or excessive fervor, you were clumsy enough to hit bottom that you've stupidly turned your hands into sand paper with all those calluses. Can you now admit that you went overboard, Ori? Can you at least do that?"

"If you order me to dig like a mole without telling me to stop, of course I'm going to hit bottom – sooner or later."

"And why did it happen sooner rather than later?"

"Because there wasn't any more ground under my feet, Boss."

"And you couldn't have noticed that in time, before it was gone?"

"I noticed it right when I hit bottom. When it was too late." Ori continues to defend himself.

"And there was no way for you to just graze the bottom, instead of hitting it?"

"Come on, Boss, don't look for excuses. It's not my fault that we've gotten to this point.

"It's not my fault either!" the Boss hysterically concludes.

"Maybe… but now, let me eat something. I'm feeling a little faint.

The Boss nods. "Me too. What are you eating, Ori?"

"Nothing, Boss."

"What do you mean, nothing? What's that? Let me taste it!"

"Damn! You never bring your own food…"

"Would you prefer me to give you an urgent order that needs to be taken care of immediately by a team made up of only you?"

Ori doesn't have a choice. "Would you like to join me, by chance?"

"Well, if you insist… just a bite, to taste it…"

"Just a bite?" Ori remarks after seeing the Boss sink his teeth into Ori's snack like an excavator does to gravel at a construction site. "Slow down! You might have no orders, but you still have an appetite. Isn't that right, Boss?"

The Boss devours the snack right under the horrified eyes of the aghast worker. Not yet content, he chugs the bottle of wine, then let's out a belch that doesn't leave room for comment, before triumphantly adding, "Don't you know that you should even thank me?"

"Really? I didn't know. Well, thank you very much, Boss," is Ori's sarcastic reply.

"The sandwich wasn't that good. I saved you the pain of having to eat it to avoid disappointing your wife. It had a strange aftertaste that I just can't pinpoint."

"I can't even say what the initial taste was like, considering I couldn't even take a bite."

"There was a nasty taste to it, trust me."

"You ate the whole thing, dammit!"

"Stopping shouting. Leave me in peace… Aaahhh…" The Boss yawns after devouring the snack, and a nap to digest his food is now a physiological necessity.

Ori, however, is appalled. "What? You have the nerve to take a nap, now?!"

"So? What's wrong with that? If you were in my shoes, wouldn't you take a moment to reflect?"

"Maybe…" Ori throws his hands in the air.

The Boss is unable to bear it any longer, so he jumps to his feet like a cricket. He's tired of being diplomatic and is set on coming to blows. "Listen, Ori, this expression that comes out of your mouth every now and then is really getting on my nerves. What the fuck does that 'maybe' mean?"

"Don't get upset, Boss," Ori says in a conciliatory tone, "if you say you're taking a 'moment to reflect,' I'm just saying that… *maybe* you are."

The Boss doesn't understand Ori's taunt. "In what sense… that *maybe* I'm not?!"

Ori is categorical and blunt in saying, "In my opinion, you're just killing time, because you don't have any more orders to give! There, I've said it!"

The Boss starts to lose his patience. "I'll tell you for the umpteenth time: the order is to await orders. Understand, or would you rather be on unemployment?"

Ori gives in at the utterance of the phrase 'unemployment,' which evokes old memories of staying home and watching TV, with his wife yelling from the kitchen, 'fix this;' 'fix that;' 'Ori, run to the supermarket;' 'Ori, wipe your ass.' "…Ok, so, we'll wait! Anyway…"

"I will wait, my friend! You just go into the pit and get back to work. Any work. March!"

Ori resigns himself to the fact. "Alright… I'll go back into the pit… I have to take a piss, anyway, Boss."

The Boss doesn't believe his own ears. "What are you intent on doing, Ori?"

"I have to take a piss, Boss."

"In the pit?"

"If not there, where?"

"You're a troglodyte, Ori… Now I know where your name comes from: from *orina* or, so it's clear to you, *urine*. You make me sick!"

"Hasn't there ever been a time when you couldn't hold it, Boss?"

"Not in the pit, Ori. Not in the pit!" shouts the Boss as he thrashes about like a robot gone mad.

Ori remains calm and doesn't react to the Boss, who, waving a fist under his nose, threatens to punch the worker. Fact is, Ori is not the type to shit his pants every time his superiors raise their voices a little. If they want to use closed fists to threaten the working class, let them. Let it be clear, though, that the gesture is historically incorrect, because a closed fist is the symbol of class struggle, not repression of legitimate personal needs – like taking a piss when it's coming out of your ears. Anyway, Ori believes the Boss is exerting himself on two levels: one, by getting upset, and the second, by getting fed up. So, with a candid, though hypocritical tone in his voice, our good worker challenges the Boss with another load of crap, "So, we have a pit that we can't piss into?"

The Boss is electrified yet again; it's like he's stepped on an exposed high voltage cable. "It's not our pit, don't you understand?! Show a little respect, dammit! It might not be our cradle but *maybe* our grave."

"You too with the 'maybes,' huh, Boss?!" Ori continues needling him, though he's cautiously knocking on wood at the same time, hoping the uncertain nature of the word *maybe* turns out to be something positive and not negative.

The Boss doesn't seem to be calming down, though, nor letting up. "*I* am authorized to ponder such serious questions. Me, yes, dammit!"

So, tired of being a doormat, Ori flat out responds, "Well, I piss on your questions and on your disgusting world, too!"

At this point, the gauntlet – no longer metaphorical, but literal – has been thrown.

"Ori, now I'm going to smash your face, because this isn't simple insubordination, but downright bad manners – not to mention you can't desecrate the pit and get away with it. Come on, put 'em up!"

Fight with the Boss? Ori doesn't think it's good idea. If he hits him, he risks really being fired. If he takes a beating, he'll still be fired, but with a steak on his eye. Ori is either screwed, or screwed and beaten to a pulp, which isn't a great alternative. So, he metaphorical pulls a rabbit out of his hat and changes the subject to buy time until a better idea comes to mind to mitigate the tension. "Hey, Boss, look what I've found as I was urinating into your pit!"

The Boss doesn't want to hear Ori carry on. "Don't change the subject. Get out of there and fight like a man, if you're even capable!"

"You know how to type, Boss?" Ori persists.

The Boss mistakes the metallic object Ori finds in the pit as a gimmick to delay the payback he's about to receive in the form of a beating.

"What's a typewriter have to do with anything? It's not like we're holding a prize fight in Las Vegas and have to type up a press release. We'll fight right here where we're standing. However, if you really want to add that commercial aspect to our boxing match, we're going to Vegas by plane, and not by car."

"I found a typewriter. Maybe some journalist threw into the pit before moving over to TV news."

"Don't assume anything, Ori. You may even find a television in the pit, but that doesn't mean it'll be the end of civilization, for heaven's sake."

"Or a refrigerator, Boss, but that doesn't mean it'll be full, for fuck's sake."

The Boss ignores the comment, because he's gotten used to his subordinate's bad language. Instead, he focuses on the object. "How about that. A typewriter turning up in age of computers… does it work?"

Ori is perplexed and scratches his head. "I don't know, take a look," he says, passing the hot potato onto the next player.

"This thing is all wet. Damn you, Ori!"

"Be patient. It'll dry, sooner or later."

Despite dripping with Ori's urine, the antique gets the Boss's attention. He tries one of the keys, and like a mini catapult, it launches a spurt of yellow liquid straight into one of Ori's eyes.

"You're right. It really is a typewriter."

"What's it good for?"

"Idiot, it's right in the name: to *write*."

"And to think, I pissed right on it."

"Inadvertently, I would hope."

"I really needed to pee, not to write, never mind to read. I only read on the toilet, when I really have to go. Reading helps you concentrate on your bowel movements, Boss, provided they're not erotic stories, complete with pictures. In that case, several bodily functions would interfere and cancel each other out. It's a real burden trying to take a crap with an erection.

The Boss, however, doesn't pay attention to Ori's reasoning. "You think like you dig, Ori: like a Neanderthal… you are pitting basic physiological needs against intellectual ones: you prefer toilet paper to the printed page…"

Ori, however, continues to grasp at straws. "Isn't hygiene a plus when it comes to our civilization?"

"Civilization, dimwit, originated with the invention of writing, not toilet paper. Is it possible you can't tell the difference between a foundation of civilization and some gimmick advertised on TV?"

Ori is forced to come to terms with his ignorance, not knowing what his boss is referring to: the toilet paper or the typewriter. He then realizes, however, it's the latter. "So, I found an archaeological artifact. How much could it be worth?" persists the damn slacker.

"Don't get any ideas. This is property of Pit Management," declares the Boss, thereby disappointing Ori.

"But I found it, dammit!" complains Ori, hemming and hawing until the Boss gives him a whack on the head, which forces him to settle down.

"Stop complaining! Whatever is found in the pit, belongs to the pit." The Boss's tone of voice doesn't permit a reply.

Ori protests in his own way, "Damn pit, I shit on you!" after which he lets out a fart in direction the ditch.

The Boss is outraged, and he threateningly grabs him by the collar. "How dare you? It's provided you with work for so long, it's given you a typewriter to express yourself intellectually, and you have the gall to treat it like that?"

"It's not like I caused a cave-in with one of my explosive atomic farts!" Ori replies to minimize the situation.

"You're an animal, that's what you are!"

Ori, however, has good reason to feel the way he does. "It's no use anymore. First, work has stalled, because the pit is done; and, second, the typewriter has been snatched up by Pit Management, even though it's not *managing* a damn thing, considering it's not sending us any further orders. As for freedom of expression… well, we're better off just forgetting about that completely!"

Ori's allusions to the 'democratic' system in the work zone causes the Boss to lose his temper yet again. "Now I'm going to draft a few orders that are going to make your hair stand on end, you moron!"

"What orders?" Ori doesn't believe him.

"I don't know… maybe the same ones as those that are coming down from the above."

"And if they come by mail, I mean, already written?"

"Then, I'll rewrite them."

"Is it really worth rewriting them, Boss?"

Ori's insinuations about the lack of orders warrant a thought-out reply, so the Boss responds by saying, "Even if they come down in person or by phone, someone from above will still have to write them up, because all orders have to appear in black and white. And I, who have a sense of duty, am going to put them in black in white beforehand. Any objections?"

"You have to insert a sheet of paper before you can put them down in black in white."

It's only at this point that the Boss notices the snag: to write with instruments from the pre-electronic age, one needs a sheet of paper.

"Ha, that's true. I was typing without paper in the roller. Funny!"

"You mean, I'm right, Boss? That would be the first time you have – more or less unofficially – given me credit for being right."

"Don't be so surprised. Fact is, my motto is: render unto Caesar that which is Caesar's…

and unto Ori, that which is Ori's – naturally. That is… Nothing!"

"That's what I thought. Thanks, Boss."

"That's my job, Ori, my job. Even if it can be so damn counter-productive to be too loyal to the regulations."

"Coming from you, Boss, that sounds strange. Wouldn't you want everyone to follow the rules, instead of urging them to sidestep the norms?"

The work zone looks like it's been abandoned by both God and the Devil. Not a buzzing fly can be heard, only the distant sound of two quibbling workers. The area is like the surface of the moon: full of craters and mounds of sand and dirt. The excavators have the air of prehistoric monsters with wide-opened jaws and sharp teeth ready to devour their prey. The cranes look like enormous winged animals balancing themselves on one leg. Everything is immobile and in a state of suspension. A satellite image of the work zone would reveal the presence of only two workers, Ori and the Boss – the first wearing an orange hardhat, the second with a blue one. Seen from above they would appear to be the flashing dots of some zany videogame. There isn't a sign of any other human presence. There are heaps of piled scrap metal and loads of harden cement, but no sounds of the screeching stone cutting grinder nor the pneumatic hammer breaking through the road to expose the earth's crust.

The Boss lowers his voice. He doesn't want prying ears to hear him. It's true that there's no one around, but one never knows…. "Think about it: if you had worked very, very slowly to buy time, there would still be a pit to finish digging. Would we have, or would we have not, both benefited from that?"

Ori, however, is more stubborn than a mule. "If I hadn't worked fast, would you have, or would you have not, fired me?"

"If you had only pretended to work fast, I would have only pretended to fire you. I would have laid you off, you would have collected unemployment benefits, then we would have started digging elsewhere, without being too obvious… One work zone here, another there… we would've made a good impression, gone through the motions and… voila! Instead…"

Ori scratches his stomach. "Instead?"

"Instead, you took it too damn seriously. You turned a normal dig, a simple moving of dirt, into an endless pit that that puts us at risk of being buried under the weight of our mutual civil, criminal, not to mention po – li – ti – cal responsibilities."

Ori doesn't give up and insists, "What the fuck!? The order was to dig a pit, and I dug it."

"But you took so much pleasure in digging that you hit bottom. So, there's nothing left to do but to fire you immediately. I'm sorry," is the sad conclusion the Boss comes to.

Ori can't believe his ears. He looks around, but there's not a living soul to be seen. The work zone is closed and airtight. Aside from himself, there isn't anyone representing the working class. Despite the enormity of the pit, and the boundless limits of the work area, he's the only one holding a pick and shovel, which foments in Ori the suspicion that the Boss is just screwing around with him. "I'm fired? Those are your final words?"

"Yes, my poor man. However, don't get down on yourself. Never give up, Ori. Don't despair, my friend. And… good luck!"

The Boss is bluffing so well, that, for a moment, Ori falls for it hook, line and sinker.

"Listen to your conscience. I've dedicated the best years of my life to the pit, giving it my all. That's why I hit bottom!"

So, the Boss speaks to him with a hand on his heart, like a father would do to a son who's somewhat of a momma's boy, "Is it possible that you don't realize the gravity of the situation?"

"What situation?" Ori's eyes widen in all their innocence.

The Boss scrutinizes Ori for a moment to figure out if the foolish worker, who isn't even worth his weight in salt as a laborer, could be jerking him around. However, once he realizes that a worker on the verge of losing his job is a being at the mercy of circumstance and, therefore, an inconsistent, if not, inexistant threat, he lets out a sigh of relief and engages the tactic of *a trouble shared is a trouble halved.*

"Ori, it's useless, it's all useless. The pit is done, and there are no other orders. I don't even know what's going to happen to me. Believe me, I took action: I tried to create work, come up with orders on my own, but it was no use. So, there's nothing left but to pack it in… and look for other work …Take my advice…" the Boss concludes, sighing.

Ori perceives a quiver in the Boss's voice, like he too doesn't consciously want to admit the state of things, and he's being grabbed at the throat by the sense of nothingness and disorientation that's in the immediate future.

"So, what will you do?" Ori asks, worried, as he intuitively realizes that the destinies of each of them are indissolubly bound together, and that they are both clinging to a same thin piece of rope to avoid falling into the abyss.

The Boss throws his hands in the air, "I'll stay here, on the front lines, and oversee the pit."

Having said this, the Boss, hands on hips, stands atop the mound of dirt Ori has dug from the ditch. All of a sudden, Ori sees the pit for what it truly is: a deep and useless empty hole. At the same time, however, a stroke of genius sparkles in Ori's eyes. "I have an idea."

"You?" The Boss is astonished.

"Yes," nods Ori with conviction, "it's strange, but true."

The Boss is skeptical; however, he knows he has nothing to lose. "Let's hear it. That way, you won't go around bad-mouthing me by telling everyone I wouldn't listen."

Ori pauses in silence for a moment in order to give the brilliant solution to the problem greater impact. "What if we were to close the fucking pit back up? Have you thought of that?"

The Boss hesitates, thinks about it: *a stupid idea is still an idea, especially when there aren't any others, dammit!* Still, he does face a serious dilemma. "We worked so hard to dig it up, and now you want to fill it in?"

Ori, however, replies without hesitation, "An open hole, the way it is, poses a danger: people could fall in and break their necks. How would that make us look?"

"That's true, too" the Boss has to admit. He scratches his head and starts biting his lip again, embarrassed by the choice facing him – a choice that fucking chatterbox, not to mention nitwit, Ori, has proposed.

Ori, feeling he has the upper hand, continues, "If someone should get hurt, the responsibility would fall on the work supervisor, Boss; meaning, you. You could run into problems, believe me, or worse, there could even be very serious consequences."

"Dammit!" exclaims the Boss, being further pushed into a corner by Ori, who demands an answer and wants him to make a choice or take a position to break the deadlock.

"You're starting to make sense a little too often, Ori!" the Boss says, though it's tough for the him to admit. "Of course, if I were in charge, I would take certain measures, or in this case, give certain orders. But my role is limited. I can't bypass the chain of command – no way. At least, I don't think so…"

"But that would be the most logical thing to do right now," Ori continues to prod him, sensing that the convictions of the person directly above him are vacillating like reeds in the wind.

"I'll bet those in charge are likely thinking the same thing," the Boss says, trying to get through the situation. Scratching his scalp, he causes a small wisp of hair to sprout atop his otherwise bald head.

"Not 'likely', Boss, they most certainly are. This time I *will* bet my ass on it!"

Ori's enthusiasm is so contagious that it elicits an initial, "Yes, you're right," which quickly turns into, "However… no, I can't take on this responsibility, it's too great for me. Pre-empt the orders? It's out of the question! If I only knew who were in charge, I could request an official and irrefutable written order that would have to be carried out!

"Then, what do you plan to do?" Ori asks impatiently.

"We'll wait a little longer," the Boss says, indecisively, "then we'll see. Only time will tell. Right? Plus, at that point, I'll know better whether

I have to really fire you or not. Just to be clear, though, in the meantime, your salary is paused."

"Fine, as long as you pause all your mental masturbation, Boss; it's melting your brain!"

The Boss, feeling his authority is being questioned, feigns calm and cold-bloodedness, so as to demonstrate some self-composure. In a familiar manner, he places a hand on Ori's shoulder. "I'll repeat for the umpteenth time that I fully understand your state of mind, but don't lose heart. An order will come down in due time. Trust me."

"As long as that order is not fire anyone or prohibit me from slacking off every now and then?" Ori whines, as he feels himself collapsing under weight of the Boss's arm that's encircling his shoulder – first in a friendly manner, then threateningly, like a noose tightening around his neck.

"Now that would be hilarious! A really great frigging joke!" the Boss laughs, savoring with pleasure the cruelty of the order that could come down at any moment: an order to walk on hot coals, to wear a crown of thorns, or one forcing Ori to spend a weekend with his mother-in-law, etcetera, etcetera.

Ori frees himself from the Boss's grip. He'd rather not even think about it. "Let's leave things alone. As the saying goes: If it ain't broken…"

"…don't fix it, Ori! Right. Let's sit on the edge of the pit and smoke a cigarette to stimulate our neurons, not to mention rouse our lungs with some harmless toxins. Anyway, with all the harmful fumes emanating from the pit, what's a fucking cigarette?"

Ori and the Boss sit with their legs dangling over the edge of the pit. The view is depressing – there's practically nothing to look at. However, Ori takes it in with his usual lower-class optimism. He has no choice but to see the positive side of the most negative things to prevent falling victim to the desperation and nihilism that would incite him to throw himself right into the pit, like the legend of Empedocles jumping into the crater of Mount Etna.

"It's nice here, don't you think?" Ori comments.

The Boss doesn't share the sentiment. When it comes down to it, he's never liked the pit. Being boss here is just another job. He could never lie to himself and simply thinks, *It would be, if only there weren't a pit, emitting an unhealthy, stinking air coming from its oozing putrid sewage.* "No, it's sickening!"

"I like the view *because* of the pit."

"I don't get you, Ori. I mean, I know you need the pit to be able to carry on your wretched earthly existence – all that digging allows you to pay your oppressive monthly bills. But, you know, there's a big difference between that and thinking the pit is a perfect example of an ideal situation.

"I know, but, unfortunately, that's a professional bias. I could almost say that I was born in the pit, and that's where I'll probably die. Though it gets deeper and deeper, it's still the same pit as that of my childhood: dark and distressing with no trace of light, a black hole, the bottom of a cave where you see shadows of an unreachable higher truth..."

Ori leaves the sentence hanging so the Boss can have his say.

"It's unreachable for those who settle for less; for those, like you, who don't want to reach it, Ori. So, there it remains, at the bottom of that cave."

It's the first time both Ori and the Boss have been personal with each other and have set aside the hierarchical chain of command. They find themselves face to face, maybe not like two old friends, but simply two men able to understand one another, even in light of their difference in rank. So, Ori speaks from the bottom of his heart and says, "Boss, you know the orders better than I do: fill in any cracks of light, seal up any openings, hinder, hamper, obstruct any hope, and dig, dig, dig… I've never had any other choice."

"It's sad, Ori."

"I'll admit that I've always had some hidden faith, though. I've often told myself: you'll see; the pit will be useful in building a solid infrastructure, a foundation for the future?"

"I doubt it, Ori."

"Me too, Boss. It was just a thought."

"A senseless thought. Listen and learn. I'm older and more experienced than you. I've seen many pits and few, very few, foundations. Maybe it's pessimism, but, unfortunately, that's the way it is."

"Maybe you're right, Boss!"

"Whatever will be, will be, Ori."

A light breeze blows in as if to seal this moment of unity and solidarity, in which two extremely diverse individuals are sitting elbow to elbow, scrutinizing the dark abyss of their common destiny: death. The breeze lifts the centuries old soil (which Ori's voracious shovel has dug up) into a rising vortex, like a flushing toilet turned upside down toward the sky, and it seems to act as a reminder that 'you came from dust, and to dust you shall return.' The fleeting moment that seems to evoke the Latin phrase, *memento mori,* is interrupted by an order that comes over the work zone loudspeaker: "JUMP TO IT!"

Ori and the Boss look at each other, terrified. "Did you hear that?" asks Ori.

"You bet I did, Ori. It almost blew out my ear drums."

"Could've it been an order?"

"Good question," mutters the Boss. "Unfortunately, I have to admit that I don't know."

"It seemed like an order to me," Ori hesitates in saying, though, because he doesn't have any upper-level responsibilities, no voice in things, and no direct knowledge of such matters, he can say whatever he likes without being contradicted by the facts.

Ori can look like an idiot under any circumstance, but the Boss, absolutely not. Considering his position, the Boss is forced to tread cautiously and be open to any possibility.

"It seemed like an order to me too, but I can't say for sure," the Boss adds. "If we obey it, and it's not an order, how will we look when one comes down that's official and by the book?"

"You don't know how to recognize an order, Boss?

"Between one order and another, yes, but knowing whether an order is official is much more difficult. Let me explain. In a certain sense, it's true that official orders are immediately identifiable: they instruct you do something or not to do something. In short, what to do and what not to do, which, in theory, seems simple."

"Good," Ori says, trying to end the discussion – he would have been much happier with a simple answer, which would have made his life a lot easier.

"However, I now have to admit that I'm a little uncertain about what to do," the Boss continues, kindling disappointment in Ori, who thinks he has already run into enough problems all morning long. "Fact is, I'm not sure what the order consists of, provided we're even talking about an order. An order that seems uncertain, might not be an order at all."

"Then what is it?" Ori naively asks.

"That's the point. Maybe it is an order, and if it's telling us to jump to it, we would be making a mistake not to do so. However, it's not a properly structured order, and orders that are not officially clear can be disobeyed."

"So, what do we do?" is the Hamletic query of the Working Class, honorably represented by Ori, the slacker.

"Let me think," says the Boss, as he raps on his head with his fist, as if he were trying to crack open a coconut to get to the milk inside. "Should we jump to it or not?"

Ori is embarrassed by the fact that the Boss's merciless banging on his forehead resounds as if the head of his direct superior were completely empty. He decides to distract the supervisor from his actions, because it's not only awkward for the Boss, but it's even unsettling for someone who is subordinate to such a 'bigshot.' So, seeing as nothing useful is going to come from Boss's head, it's pointless to waste time waiting for some stroke of genius.

"Excuse me, Boss, but what are the orders good for, anyway?"

The Boss's thoughts on this topic are pretty clear, though. "To obey. Orders are given to be followed. Don't make me lose track of my thoughts."

"Why do you have to think about it so much?"

"Why are you asking me what to do, if you already know, then?"

It's just that there are way too many choices, Boss. One: to jump to it. Two: not to jump to it.

"Don't piss me off, Ori! I repeat, if the order were clear, we wouldn't have trouble choosing a side.

"Left, or right?"

"Those are driving directions, I'm talking about how to proceed, and that's where the first logical doubt comes into play. If we were to desert the center… of the pit, and leave it to the mercy of itself, you know what would happen? Instead of an order, we would have disorder. An order that directly results in disorder has to be balanced with an appropriate counter-order. Understand?"

"So, we shouldn't jump to it?" Ori asks, still racked with the fact that he doesn't understand a fucking thing, provided there is even something to understand.

"No, we should not jump to it!" the Boss booms. "We can't jump to it, because if we do, we'd be following the order, but we would also be disobeying the counter-order that's surely about to come down; there's no doubt about that, you can bet your ass on it."

"Are you sure?" Ori says distrustfully.

"Trust me," is the Boss's official reply.

"So, we shouldn't make a move?"

"No. We'll stay right here and wait for more precise orders. Besides, that frightful ditch isn't going anywhere…"

"If you say so…" Ori frowns, revealing some harboring doubt he has about the Boss's ability to solve the problem quickly and completely.

"Yes, I say so. My word should be enough for you."

Ori is irritated. Quite frankly, he doesn't expect such a bossy attitude after the moment of corporate solidarity they shared. It's like they had been in an imaginary friendly embrace on the edge of the abyss. Right when they were finally more familiar with one another, able to commiserate about their mutual anguish and agreeing on how truly deceptive existence is, out comes that damn superior tone of voice again in line with his place in the chain of command. It would be one thing if he were at least good at being in charge, dammit!

The Boss now regrets having been so familiar with a subordinate, having shared fragments of his personal life, not to mention professional concerns, which he would have been better off keeping to himself. You never know. If Ori were fired, he could use the information to blackmail and cast the Boss in a bad light in the eyes of management, which would certainly demand a detailed report of the situation. So, in the hopes Ori hasn't already mentally recorded his thoughts, the Boss tries to sidetrack the conversation by bringing up a topic of secondary importance.

"Cigarette?"

"No thanks, I have my own," Ori says, misunderstanding the Boss's words, which could have meant anything at all, other an act of generosity.

"That's exactly what I meant: give me one of yours, Ori. If you don't mind."

"I should have known!" Ori complains. Then, like a wild horse that has been tamed, he holds out the pack and adds, "Please, help yourself…"

"Give me a light, my friend," the Boss says in a heartening manner, while crumbling up the pack after having taken the last cigarette. "Give me a light."

The Boss inhales deeply, then let's out a cloud of smoke right in Ori's face, who justly feels he is being mocked.

"That was the last one, Boss. Let's split it, if you don't mind."

"Where is it written," the Boss objects, "that we have to split it? The only thing written on the pack is *Smoking can kill.* So, you should thank me, Ori, because if you survive the firing, you'll have an extra day to live, partly due to me having forced you to smoke one less cigarette."

"Or maybe an extra day of suffering."

"Worse for you!"

This doesn't sit well with Ori. "That's not fair, and I don't like it at all!" Ori bursts out, raising the shovel more with the intention of throwing it over his shoulder and getting the hell out of there, rather than as a threatening gesture.

However, the action has an unexpected effect: the Boss instinctively raises his arms to defend himself from the shovel Ori is aggressively waving in front of him. *How about that*, Ori thinks, *he's scared of me. Once in a while, the Boss is actually afraid of* me.

"What do you intend to do with that shovel? Hit me in the head? Put it down, right now, otherwise you'll regret such a rash decision," shouts the Boss.

Ori, however, gnashes his teeth like a dog whose bone has just been snapped from its jaws. It doesn't seem Ori wants to give up taking justice into his own hands, instead of going through the normal bureaucratic process of filing a complaint, which is never taken seriously, because of the Boss's abuse of power. Ori understands that if he wants to finally break the Boss's head with the shovel – or break the shovel by hitting the Boss's head – he'll have to do it now. This would be the right moment to squash him like a cockroach, dammit!

"I'm sorry, Boss, when something's due, it's due."

The Boss curls up, his hands covering his head to blunt the imminent blow, however, right at the precise moment Ori is about to strike, another commanding "JUMP TO IT!" comes from above, paralyzing the worker.

The Boss composes himself, while Ori remains fossilized in the position of attack that he previously assumed. "Now look what you've done, bigshot, with your, 'So, we shouldn't make a move?'"

"Then, should we jump to it, Boss?"

"I've already said no, Ori, so please don't insist."

Ori throws the shovel into the pit: *I can never catch a break. Just when I decide to take action, I have to immediately slam on the brakes, come to my senses, and act like there's nothing wrong,* he thinks.

The Boss is ready forgive and forget. Ori's threatening attitude is now water under the bridge, just a bad memory in history of labor relations, a futile and spiteful corporate squabble more worthy of a verbal scolding than a report to Pit Management. All the same, the Boss wants to be crystal clear.

"Now that we've already established a course of action," he continues, "we can't go back on everything just out of mental laziness or the simple fear of inconveniencing someone, dammit! We agreed on the fact that the order has to be clear and simple – without any obscurity or gray areas – for us to consider it a bona fide order. Right?"

"Exactly right!" Ori agrees, now willing to do anything to win over the Boss and have him forget the hint of defiance he showed a short while prior.

"Then, we can't jump to it after the second 'jump to it', without explaining why we didn't jump to it after the first 'jump to it,' right?"

"Right, because we didn't jump to it at all?"

"Because there wasn't anything to jump to. At least, that's what we decided. Now we have to stick to our understanding of things if we don't want to seriously contradict our previous inaction, which we wouldn't be able to explain at all, dammit! I don't know if I'm making myself clear, Ori."

Dialectics isn't one Ori's strongpoints. He's not able to grasp things that are overly theoretical. He's a man of the shovel – the pick and shovel – or else the pneumatic hammer. He's not a man of intellect, so he gives a proletariat nod of his head. In that, the Boss infers a gesture of moral complicity, mistaking a simple 'what do I know?' for a 'look at them, how can they allow such bullshit to happen!'

"That way, they'll learn not to give us senseless orders," the Boss decrees, convinced he's speaking for both of them, though he really doesn't have a clue about anything at this point.

All Ori has to do now is show a glimmer of mental activity by pretending to have an opinion of his own on the matter. "With all due respect, though, orders shouldn't be contested."

"Orders shouldn't be contested? Coming from me, that would be valid, coming from you, it's just crap," the Boss replies, stopping him short.

This doesn't sit well with Ori, so he asserts the right to his opinion, though he's not able to express any logical concept that's worthy of a child above the age of three.

"And why is that?"

"What do you mean, why?" The Boss doesn't let him off easy this time around. "You're already getting a big head? Have you forgotten that I'm the Boss around here? It's my job to decide which orders are valid and which are not; those that need further clarification, and those that are just blatantly inapplicable and counter-productive."

"As long as you don't blame me for not wanting to jump to it."

"Did you jump to it? No. So, what do you want from me? When it comes down to it, you didn't follow orders."

"Right, because you precisely told me not to."

"And, if told you to jump in lake, would you have obeyed that order, too?" The Boss lets out a laugh.

Ori seriously ponders the comment about the lake. Then, however, his poor idiotic mind spawns a slightly more thought-out response.

"Now I understand: you want to throw me off guard. You're going to jump to it, while at the same time telling me not to, so that I'm left looking like a slacker. But I'm not falling for it, Boss, because I'm going to jump to it before you do."

"Then, I too am going to jump to it, buffoon."

Ori crouches like a sprinter on the starting blocks.

"What are you doing, Ori? What are you planning on jumping to?"

"I don't know, Boss, you tell me."

"How would I know?"

"The worst thing that can happen to worker is to end up with a Boss with no orders," Ori whines.

"Why is that?"

"Because I have to obey, but I don't know what. We're running around and jumping to it every damn day, but in the end, nothing changes. It's all the same as before."

"In the meantime, obey me. That's your goal in life."

The Boss then turns on his heels, wanting to end the discussion, and he starts to walk away while attempting to maintain a military-like posture. However, following not one, two, but three stiff and upright steps, the Boss is hit with Ori's hot-headed reply.

"You, Boss, are not an order!"

The Boss stops. He slowly turns. What the fuck! The audacity of Ori, who is shaking his head like a moron, is enough to push the Boss over the edge.

"Watch it, because you can't obey orders without a boss."

"Well, you can't obey a boss without orders."

"What makes you so sure I really don't have any?"

"Because if you had any, you would have already given them."

"The problem is that you're always looking for something that doesn't exist."

"No! The problem is my reasoning is right on the money!" Ori throws down the gauntlet, but there's nothing to challenge. The Boss has been cornered in a ring with no way out – to use a boxing term – and he's starting to run out of replies; not only those that are well-grounded, which have dried up long ago, but even just something simple and basic to say.

So, the Boss treads cautiously. "Yes, alright, but let's calm down. Let's all calm down, understand? You're enjoying being on the other side of the fence – that is, the side of being right – just a little too much. Know your place, understand? Heel, boy!"

Ori doesn't lose spirit. "Seeing as I have to heel like dog, why don't you even throw me a bone? I know how be a guard dog, too…"

"Just wait for the orders, dammit. If they instruct you to be a dog, you're authorized to be a dog. You can even wag your tail and snap at people who grab it. Happy?"

"And lift my leg?"

"Nowhere near the pit, though."

"Is that an order, Boss?"

"Go fuck yourself, Ori!"

Ori almost regrets flustering the Boss, because when it comes down to it, he is still his superior. So, he tries to mitigate the situation. "Are you upset with me? What I did do? I was only joking around!"

The Boss is pouting. He's looks like he's ready to burst into tears.

"You've gotten me into trouble, you idiot. 'Hey Boss, we've hit bottom, you have other orders to give?' Where do expect me to get them, huh? Jackass! You've brought my job into question and have jeopardized my leadership with that foolhardy attitude of yours. You shouldn't have done that, Ori, you shouldn't have asked me for orders that are just not coming down from above. I don't have any orders, understand? I don't have any! And I don't know how to get out of this tough situation. You think this isn't frustrating for me, too? I'm tired of being the boss, Ori."

"You're tired of giving orders, and I'm tired of following them, so we're even, Boss."

"We're even, Ori," the Boss dolefully agrees. The wind lifts a cloud of dust from the pit. In the midst of the vortex, which suddenly takes form and tries to sweep them away, Ori and the Boss would like to throw their arms around each other, firmly cement themselves on the ground and fend off the fury of the elements. What a nice gesture that would be, they both think, as opposed to being angry with one another. Just moments ago, they were ready to strangle each other to death. However, after running the risk of coming to blows, they would now like to be bound in solidarity, united like two trunks of the same tree sending their branches spiraling into the sky.

Another stronger burst of wind, full of sand, forces them squint, so they don't immediately perceive the quiet after the storm. They don't immediately notice the immense silence that seems to dominate the pit, which just a minute earlier was blaring like a trumpet caused by the current of air. The updraft subsided as quickly as it rose from the bowels of the Earth. Ori tries to move. He sticks his little finger in his ear to clear out the sand and dust, but he is only able to reach the first layer of wax that is shielding the residue blown in by the gale.

So, as quickly as a flash bulb, immortalizing the image of Ori picking his ear and the Boss scratching his head, the long awaited, terrifying and feared order comes down again. It has been so long since they last heard it that both men's tympanic membranes have become unaccustomed to the booming power of the command.

"JUMP TO IT!"

They flinch, breaking the imaginary embrace they adopted in a moment human weakness.

"Dammit, Boss, we shouldn't have let our guard down, we should've stayed alert. We should've known this was coming and prevented it."

"They let the bridle out a little, then all sudden they pull back on the reins with unimaginable force. Bastards!"

"Yeah! We don't even have time to enjoy a little healthy anarchy, a little homemade chaos, then all of a sudden from the disorder comes the order to 'jump to it.' Does that seem fair to you?

"No, Ori, it doesn't seem fair! This 'jump to it' is even starting wear me down."

"I'm not going to jump to it."

"Me neither."

"JUMP TO IT!" the voice insists.

"Hell! This time they really mean it, Boss!"

"You're right. It seems up there, higher up, way higher up, they're making a great effort!

"So, should we just jump to it?"

"Jump to it, Ori, jump to it!"

CHAPTER TWO

The Ten Commandments According to Ori

"The First Commandment," Ori decrees: "Don't create anyone who doesn't expressly ask to be created. How's that, Boss?"

"That's obvious, you dolt."

"The Second Commandment: If You just can't stop creating, then make sure Your creatures are happy, because loneliness is a really horrible thing. Don't use them as puppets for Your own entertainment, and above all, make sure they don't find a hostile world when You bring them into it. Always remember that the world is a part of Your Creation, and if it's a disgusting place, the same can be said for Your entire body of work – and, as a humble laborer, I ask *You*, the Greatest Artisan of all: how would that look?"

"Careful, Ori, you're talking about the Chief Executive Officer."

"Well, when it's necessary, it's necessary. The Third Commandment: Don't invent strange tales that do not exist neither in Heaven nor on Earth; that is, don't present justifications like original sin as an excuse to blame us for Your mistakes. If Creation turned out bad, or imperfect, that's fine; just come down from that pedestal, be straight with us, and say: 'My God, everyone, I've made a mess of things,' or 'The project was badly planned out,' or 'Some foolish angels put their hands on things without telling Me.' Then follow up with an, 'Anyway, whatever the case may be, let's everyone roll up our sleeves and try to make things work!'"

"Go on, Ori! the Boss encourages him. "What you said about 'rolling up our sleeves and trying to make things work' is not completely off the mark."

"Boss, the Fourth Commandment is: Don't bury Your head in the sand and adopt the policies of an ostrich. Don't pretend You're not there and are offended that Adam noticed Eve, instead of Your beard, which looks like something a seventy-eight-year-old philosopher would grow. Above all, don't stay up there in the clouds waiting for things to fix themselves on their own. Tell us what You need, how You want things, and when You want them. We, mortals, don't have time for games. Life in this disgusting pit is too damn short and complicated. So, don't You too start with riddles, parables, trivia, contests and prizes with slogans like: *How to Win an All-Expenses-Paid Vacation to Heaven.* I mean, in short, if You have something important to say, shout it out loud and clear, instead of using others as Your go-betweens – otherwise keep quiet. We'll understand things on our own; we're not stupid down here."

"Wow! You're doing great, Ori. I'm almost starting to root for you. The Fifth Commandment!"

Ori clears his voice. "Don't do unto us, Your humble Creatures, that which you wouldn't want to be done unto You. We were made in Your image – some more than others – so we all have the same rights and responsibilities. If we really are Your children, give us a weekly allowance and pay for college, like we do with our kids, instead of getting upset because we've tasted the fruit of the tree of knowledge. I mean, don't bust our chops if You have to pay for our textbooks. As for sex, which You created to lure us into temptation, close one eye if one of our hands should stray a little. Shouldn't You, as father, jump for joy when we, the sons and daughters who are financially dependent on You, want to leave the nest and start a family of our own?"

"I've always said I didn't hire an idiot. The Sixth Commandment…"

Ori is on a roll, and no one can stop him, not even Jesus Christ himself.

"Don't tell us tall fairy tales. For example, Your story of Heaven on Earth being like an amusement park is ridiculous, while the depiction of us being resurrected only to face Judgement Day, with all due respect, is a little gruesome. I ask myself: will my resurrected body look like me when I was young, or like me now, twenty kilos overweight? And, though a frightening thought, will my mother-in-law have to be reborn, and with her complete set of false teeth? Couldn't You do without creating such a ghastly sight? In any case, if Your main goal is to have my mother-in-law resurrected, with or without her false teeth, then I withdraw myself from Your divine plan."

"Ori, you amaze me! You're almost done… just try not to get a big head and get these last ones right. We've reached The Seventh Commandment… concentrate!"

Ori doesn't have to concentrate. The commandments are flowing forth more from his heart than from his head – like a raging river.

"You created pain, so find a cure. You created famine and misery, so find a cure. You created disease, so find a cure. You created my mother-in-law, so find for cure that too.

"The Eighth, and third to last Commandment! Go, you're on a roll!"

"Don't think that You are better than us! If You are, then show us, and if You can't, then back off. Anyway, always remember: that which is good for us, should be also good for You – even more so. Also, stop making little models of Heaven and The Kingdom of God; instead, try to help us by giving a coat of paint to this filthy pit. Besides, You have tons of angels sitting around twiddling their thumbs from morning to night. Make them sweat a little like You make us sweat, because here my Friend, You can't play favorites.

"The Ninth Commandment, Ori. You're on the verge of victory. Do you know that?"

"Don't terrorize us with Hell, like it's a place You've lost control of and no longer falls under Your jurisdiction. Remember that the world You've created is hell in itself, and You're primarily responsible.

"The Tenth and last Commandment, Ori. Don't disappoint me as you cross the finish line of the Biblical Tablets…"

"Keep in mind that we're not a TV show or movie, or a circus full of clowns and lions. Humanity doesn't need some superintendent or security guard keeping an eye on us. If You created us, then trust us, too. Call off Your guard dogs, and stop them from barking at us."

"Is that it, Ori?"

"For now, Boss. Did you forget to write something down?"

"What you mean, write things down, you idiot?! Who do you take me for, Moses? This was just a *diversion* to pass away the time while we wait for the orders to come down."

"*Detergent* is for dirty laundry, Boss, not to pass away the time."

"Forget about dirty laundry, Ori, which, by the way, should not be washed in public."

Ori is speechless. The day, which started badly by hitting the bottom of the pit, is threatening to come to a worse end with the intermittent order to 'jump to it,' which can neither be ignored nor taken seriously – just like the commandments that have vanished into thin air with the sound of his voice; words he no longer even recognizes.

"So, what do we do now?" Ori says, returning to the same dilemma as before.

"Well, now that we have at least mentally jumped to it, we should rest a bit. Agreed?"

"Even He rested on the seventh day, Boss."

"We'll take a break, provided you don't *rest* too much on your laurels, Ori."

"I'll do my best, Boss," Ori promises as he lies down to enjoy a few minutes of a well-deserved pause.

CHAPTER THREE

Into the Pit

The Boss surprises Ori, who is sitting on the edge of the pit contemplating the fleeting minutes and how quickly his salary is spent. His money is like the sand in an hourglass, and it's gone quicker than passing time, or time that passes – however you want to look at it.

"What's going on here?"

"Nothing, Boss."

"What do you mean, *nothing*? The Boss harshly asks.

"I was just thinking about some personal things," Ori acknowledges.

"Nice!" the Boss emphasizes. "And does this seems the right time for that? We all have our own personal affairs to think about, but we don't ponder them on the job and mix them with the business of others. Everyone's personal affairs should never be put into the same… what was I going to say… oh, fuck it… no, no, no… *bucket* is what I wanted to say. See how you make me talk! They are never put into the same bucket with other people's problems."

"It's just a quick cigarette break," Ori finally says.

"A cigarette-break?" The Boss is taken aback. "You've already taken a cappuccino-break, a snack-break, a lunch-break, a coffee-break, an after-coffee-espresso-chaser-break. So, there is no cigarette-break."

"I'm going to take one, anyway," stubbornly insists Ori.

"Then, you're going to skip the general work-break, right?"

"Right, I'll skip that… because there's no more work to do, anyway."

"What are you saying, Ori?" The Boss loses his temper, not believing his own ears.

"I'm just saying that I finished digging the pit: look at that hole."

"Finished?"

"Fi – nish – ed!" Ori highlights the fruits of his labors.

The Boss bursts out in sarcastic laughter. "You're so naïve, Ori!"

"Why's that, Boss?" The worker is amazed, as his hoists himself up with the shovel handle, which seems to have become a body limb – though not his worst appendage – rather than a tool.

"Because you never finish digging a pit – the more you dig, the closer it gets to becoming what it really should be: deep."

"Well, shit, I've finished it!"

The Boss is dumbfounded. "When?"

"A little while ago."

"Well, shit, you couldn't have warned me ahead of time?"

"I was going to, right after my snack, but I dozed off."

"So, on your list of priorities, I come after your cigarette-break?"

"Even after my coffee-break, for that matter!"

"Skip it, dammit. What do you say we go down and have look… to be sure it's really finished?"

Ori doesn't bat an eye. "If you insist. Be my guest."

"You first, Ori," the Boss deviously proposes. "I'll be right behind…"

"No. Forget about being 'right behind.' And don't even think of telling me to 'harness up and get going.' You think I'm nuts?!"

"Stop contradicting me. You know it's not worth it. Get down into the pit. That's an order, and when I give an order, you have to follow it, whether you like it or not – immediately: meaning, right away, on the spot, on your two feet, and without batting an eye. Understand?

Of course, Ori is not that easily intimidated. "You go first, Boss… please, be my guest."

The Boss, livid and resentful, furiously stomps the ground like a bull in an arena.

"Not on your dried-up dead grandmother's soul, I will. Why should I go first?"

"Because you come before me," Ori replies with angelic calmness. "Boss means he who's first in line. So, bosses, like you, go first, and then… those poor bastards like me follow."

"He who's first in line isn't the one who goes first into the pit," the Boss clarifies, "otherwise, I would be that poor bastard. Get your facts straight! It's written in the work regulations and in your contract: 'Ori, being Poor Bastard Number One, always goes in first.'"

Ori sighs. He's always reminded of his destiny as a subordinate. So, he summarizes things by saying, "I'll bet I have to be the first one in and, no doubt, the last one out, being 'Poor Bastard Number One' that I am."

The Boss has a fiendish grin on his face. "See, you're not that stupid. Now you understand what it means to be the Boss. It's exhausting, believe me."

"I can imagine. I only know what it's like being Ori!" he dolefully complains, feeling like a doormat with the weight of his social condition walking over it.

The Boss, however, is unrelenting. He doesn't let up now that he's sunk his fangs into the living flesh of the worker. "Really? And what does it mean to be Ori, in your opinion. Come on! Enlighten me! Surprise me with something intelligent that explains who you are and why you are working in this pit – if you're able to."

"Ori comes from Orestes, Boss. I'll bet you didn't know that."

"You sure it doesn't come from *orina*, you know, urine?"

"No, Boss, Ori comes from Orestes not *orina*."

"How do you know for certain?"

"I know, because I watch all the quiz shows on TV. Orestes is Agamemnon and Clytemnestra's last-born child... Electra's brother..."

"Then, you should have been an electrician, Ori, and not a general laborer. Truth is, one never knows what to ask from a type like you: Electricity? Water? Gas? Masonry? Gardening?... No. You're only good for digging ditches. That's the bitter reality of your useless existential condition," the Boss grumbles.

Now and then, the Boss really has a way of busting someone's chops.

"Excuse me, Boss, but what do you mean by 'existential condition?'"

"I'm talking about your life, stupid. Don't you understand that?"

"Don't stick your nose in my life," Ori objects, covetous of his privacy.

"I'm meddling because, professionally, you're a projection of your outward life."

Ori looks at the Boss inquisitively.

"You are a jack of all trades and a master of none," the Boss continues. "In short, you get along in life the way you do at work. You're a disaster! A catastrophe! A mess!"

"Are you talking about me?" Ori is amazed.

"Yes, you, Ori. You pick up things here and there, in a disorganized way, in the hopes of using them to answer correctly on some million-dollar quiz show, or to be capable of solving some complicated technical problem with the simple tap of a hammer. That, however, jeopardizes your work output. That's right, because if you're good with a shovel, you're always better with a hoe. And if you're good with a hoe, you're always better with a shovel. And, if you make the terrible decision of using a useless screwdriver to make an urgent repair, you'll find yourself unsurpassed in the ability to use a hacksaw. You dig ditches, but, shit, you're a complete failure at it, unfortunately. So, you might as well resign yourself to the facts and forget about Orestes…which doesn't suit you… and forget about your sister Orina, too…"

"Electra!" Ori clarifies. "Zeus transformed her into a comet after the fall of Troy."

He shouldn't have said anything. Ori shouldn't have ever pronounced the name of the city of Aeneas, of beautiful Helen and Anchises, because the Boss quickly takes advantage of the slip.

"The Fall of Troy! Ha, that's a fitting city for your sister, because she's so easy, she'll sleep with the first man she sees – just like Helen did. I wouldn't expect anything less from her."

"But Boss…" Ori would like to cite from some textbook he studied in elementary school, but that wouldn't even make sense, because he didn't do anything there but slack off.

"No *buts*! Just get it in your head that you are going into the pit first – that same pit you just finished digging with such excessive determination."

"You're blaming me for being devoted to my job?"

"Shame on you, Ori. You not supposed to work that way. When all is said and done, you have to think about each of our vested interests: yours, which is to dig, and mine, which is to give you orders to dig. It's embarrassing to have to constantly watch your back and cover your ass, so I don't end up with my face flat on the ground, because of your human and artisanal stupidity! How do you think I'm going to look in the eyes of Pit Management with you digging a ditch like that, when only a little hole in the asphalt was necessary to lay two simple sewer pipes. We're talking about a sewer, Ori, Orestes, Orina, or whatever you want to be called, and not an underground temple to one of your occult gods."

"Amen," Ori sighs, somewhat relieved.

"Get down into the pit, Ori. I've lectured you enough for now."

But Ori doesn't move.

"What's wrong. Haven't I said enough? Why are looking at me like you're a living and breathing question mark? My God, you're a hard nut to crack; even harder than the bottom of the pit."

"Can I say one thing, Boss?"

"Provided it's just one, Ori."

"A trait of any self-respecting boss is that of setting a good example, at least until that theory has been proven wrong."

"What are you trying to say?"

Ori weighs his words before speaking. "Are you sure you're a self-respecting Boss?"

"What kind of question is that!? Of course I am!"

"Then, set a good example, as laid out by the unwritten norms of common sense."

"And how can I set a good example for someone like you?"

"Simple: by going into the pit first," is Ori's logical reasoning.

"So, according to you, that would be 'setting a good example?'"

"Oh, yes," Ori confirms.

"You're so naïve, you poor imbecile. Things are not as simple as you think. You see, my friend, it's not me who's holding back. I'd be willing to go first, just to show you I'm not afraid of the dark, if nothing else. What's stopping me is the awareness that I am indispensable, being the person you directly report to. You understand? I'm not going in first for your own good. You should thank me. Unfortunately, though, there's no gratitude in your heart, which is as hard as stone… So, after you, Ori…"

With his back against the wall at this point, Ori only feels able to express himself by letting out a provocatory raspberry.

"Enough, ditch-digger. It's my duty to inspect the pit, just as it's your job to give me the all clear to do so."

"Can't we at least flip to decide who goes in first?"

"Not on your life." The Boss opposes the idea. "I have no intention of entrusting my decisions to the whims of fate, Ori, and certainly not to a game of chance. Besides, you dug it, so if you don't want to go in first, it's a sign that you don't trust your own work. Did you follow my directives?"

"Of course. I wouldn't done it any other way!"

"You didn't create some strange mess down there, did you?

"Me, create a strange mess? No one gave me that order."

"Good. Then, show me the faith you have in your work by checking things out first."

"No, no, no. I'm afraid of the unknown, Boss."

"I doubt you dug so deep as to reach the unknown; at least I hope not," the Boss says, amazed. "So, get down into the pit, right now! March!"

"Who's going to make me?" Ori replies, expressing his displeasure.

"The chain of command that issues the orders, that's who. The boss only gives those orders and simple workers like you…"

"…constantly get screwed," Ori complains without mincing words. "Why should I beat around the bush when I'm jeopardizing my own ass by going down into that fucking bottomless pit?" As Ori utters these words, he leans over the edge of the ditch, but he freezes at the sight of the void below him. His face loses all its complexion.

"What's down there?" The Boss says, trying to urge him on. "Why are you so pale?"

"What in the world? Boss, it's really deep!"

"Leave the world out of it, Ori, it hasn't done anything to you that's really bad or painful – yet. You're still do for a real kick in the ass. You'll feel it when it gets here.

"Yet? Well, that's comforting… Who knows what the world has in store for me to finish its work of destroying a human being. It's been ruthless to me all my life; there's never been a glimmer of hope, a flicker of a bright future. You know what tomorrow holds for me?"

"I can only imagine; a bill that's overdue? Spare me the trifles, Ori! I repeat, all things considered, no one has yet tried to completely destroy your existence. The world is only giving you an initial, small taste of its wickedness. It's only grazing the surface; the real bombardment is still waiting to hit you on the head!"

"I curse the day I was born."

"You should have thought of that sooner. Now it's too late. Go on, Ori, get going. You have my corporate blessing and all my human and professional sympathy. What do you want? What more do you want?" The Boss pauses. "Why are you standing as still a pole… like the sister of your namesake, what's his name, Orestes…"

"Electra?"

"Right. I wanted to say light pole, but I guess electric pole would be more appropriate. Come on, drop the ladder…"

"I repeat, my only fault is having been born into this world," Ori says in anguish as he lets the ladder unroll into the pit.

"You're such a pain in the ass, Ori! I was born into this same world. And, just like me, so were millions of other human beings, who are also, more or less, justified in complaining about whoever created them. It's useless to get so upset about it."

"It might be useless, but when someone has his pockets as full as me."

"Your pockets full? Don't make me laugh. When have your pockets ever been full?"

"Of problems, I mean," Ori replies, clarifying his financial situation.

"Ah," the Boss acknowledges, "but you're not saying anything new with your justified, though much too random, complaints. Though, you know what they say; a problem shared is a problem halved. So, when it comes to your salary and your existence, just live with it, like everyone else has to – me, first and foremo…

never mind, I'll put myself second. Where do we stand, Ori?"

"I'm getting ready to go down."

"So, go. What are you waiting for? We don't have any more time to waste."

"Am I insured, Boss?"

"Don't bust my shops, Ori. *Insure*, rather, that you are securely connected to the cable… Get going. I understand your need for security – job and social security – but being too needy will cripple you."

"No, breaking my neck will cripple me."

"Do you have your hardhat on? Yes? Then you're following all work zone regulations. Whatever happens, it can't statistically be considered as the umpteenth case of death in the workplace, but rather a just trivial work accident widely found in the daily newspapers. Don't let what happens in other work zones scare you, Ori – here, I'm in charge."

"That's exactly what scares me, Boss."

"If I say nothing will happen to you, nothing should happen to you… theoretically. Trust me."

"Go tell to that to everyone I owe money to. Then, if they trust you…"

"You're always going on and on, you chickenshit!" the Boss huffs and puffs, fed up with such a foolish quarreler.

Ori changes the subject, realizing he's not going make any progress on the topic. "It's not me that's going on and on, it's the ladder that's going deeper and deeper!"

The Boss doesn't let things go and throws salt into the wound. "It's going deeper and deeper now, because you continued to dig and dig earlier."

"And I still owe money to lots of people. Maybe it would be better if I were to hide down there forever."

"Don't be stupid. Your creditors would start asking me about you," the Boss replies, shutting him up.

On the inside of the pit, Ori's body is swinging on the rope ladder, looking like a man hanging from a noose, or the pendulum of a cuckoo clock that can't keep time.

"And would you give me up? Answer. Don't leave me hanging over an abyss of doubt with no corporate ground under my feet."

"I hired you, so you also owe me… a debt of gratitude," the Boss replies, worsening the heavy state of mind weighing on Ori – his ass swinging in the breeze – as if famished creditors were waiting for him at the bottom of the pit, like a pack of infernal guard dogs.

"What does that mean?" Ori's voice – as tense as the ropes supporting him – echoes from the pit.

"It means that even *I* am one of your creditors, my friend. Anyway, how do you plan on running away from it all?"

"But I don't owe you money," Ori replies, feeling the need to clarify the type of debt he owes him.

"It was hyperbole, Ori."

"I'm not even going to ask what hyperbole means, because I have bad about feeling about it."

"Don't worry, hyperbole isn't dangerous. Whistle when you get to the point, as you should."

"Get to the point?"

"It's an expression, you brute – when you reach the point, the bottom!" the Boss emphasizes, surprised that Ori can't put two and two together… "Don't you even know an expression when you hear one?

"It's not a question of the language, Boss, it's the terminology. We're not on the same wavelength, so we're having a hard time verbally communicating. We're using completely different expressive codes, even if they are *somewhat* similar. I'm speaking *Ori* and you're speaking *Boss*."

The Boss is suddenly suspicious; there's something fishy going on here.

"This is not you talking, Ori. These are phrases you've surely heard at some union meeting. But you should know that you're only dealing with words you don't fully understand, and that they've been fed to you on purpose to further confuse your petty ideas."

"Truth is, you confused me a lot more with that stupid 'to the point,'" Ori sharply objects, not wanting to always be perceived as the fool.

The Boss's eyes widen, surprised at such an insult that, in his opinion, is damaging to his professional dignity.

"My 'to the point' is stupid? I'm going to note that… Anyway, I repeat, what I meant was, whistle as soon as you reach the bottom, when you reach that *point,* the summit of your descent! Do you understand now? A clear and simple whistle – or do I have to put you on report?"

In the midst of such a rough descent, Ori's mind isn't clear enough to reason things out, and his queries risk being redundant. "You mean the kind of whistle I make with my two fingers?"

"Any kind of whistle, you dog!" the Boss replies, losing his patience.

"Whistle… Dog… Got it."

"You didn't understand a fucking thing, Ori. You have to whistle to me, not to a dog. Understand?"

"To you. Got it… Now I'm going to descend a little more… I'll go down a little at a time until I eventually reach the bottom."

However, much time passes, it flies, or rather it completely dissipates, like Ori's salary does before the end of month, but still nothing. The Boss looks into the pit to see how far Ori has gotten.

"So, have you reached the fucking bottom or not?"

It's only after a brief pause that Ori, not liking the darkness around him, sends up a corroboratory, "Yes, Boss."

"Then, why didn't you whistle like I said?" the Boss asks, wanting an explanation.

"I couldn't whistle with my two fingers, because my hands are shaking too much. I know I dug this ditch, the but darkness down here is still frightening. I did let out a little bit of a whistle, though – like that of a robin."

"Robin's chirp, they don't whistle, you fraud! There's a big difference between whistling with your two fingers and a robin's chirp, Ori. You expect a faint bird call to reach me up here? Do you know why some robins are red? Because when they emit their mating calls, their chirps, they blush from embarrassment. And you! You're not even mortified to imitate that kind of sound? I'm going to give you a reason to stop screwing around with me…

"But I wasn't making any kind of sexual bird sound, I was just calling up to you."

"The only thing missing today was for you to try to get my attention by using a crude sexual mating call, probably hoping I'd be lured in – hook, line and sinker – and respond by chirping back down to you. Don't get any funny ideas."

Ori can' take it any longer. He was sent to the bottom of the pit, in pitch darkness, and he doesn't even know exactly why he was told to go down there. "Damn all bosses and whoever gave them work!"

From the top of the pit, the Boss overhears Ori's words. "I heard everything, loud and clear. Now, I am going to put you on report. You said I, like all bosses, am a 'jerk.'"

"I said 'work' not 'jerk,' Boss. Someone must have hired you… and, yes, I'm upset with that person, and with whoever put you above me, but not with you personally, my direct superior."

"See how stupid you are? No one put me above you, it's you who have descended below me."

"Well, I didn't descend willingly."

"So, it was me who forced you to go down there? No, Ori, I simply convinced you, by using the intellect that assists me in my position of high authority, a position of hierarchical superiority. I'm one person, just like you, but I'm worth double in comparison. Why don't you use your brain: if you can't or are unable to whistle, use your voice and shout up to me, 'Hey, Boss, I've reached the bottom!'"

"But you told me to whistle." Ori whines.

"And if I had told you to take flying leap into the pit, would you have done that too?"

"Now I'm going to come back up there and start smacking you around!"

"No, Ori, now that you're down there, there's no need for you to come back up. Avoid any acts of force, like the instinctual force of habit of coming back up without permission, which you would bitterly regret. Maybe I'll just come down there, and lower myself to your level. Hold the ladder, Ori, I'm coming to inspect the pit."

"No one held it for me when I came down. The feeling of my very survival hanging in air made me doubt my own class consciousness. And a worker without class consciousness is like a drunken acrobat."

"When we climb back up, I'll go first. That way, we'll be even, and we will have followed work regulations. Your class consciousness happy now, or is it still up in arms, scandalized by such social inequality?"

"Nice work regulations: I'm sure they were written by someone who loves giving orders – like you."

"What do you mean by that? They're not impartial enough?"

"What I want to say is when all is said and done, it's always us who get screwed."

"Stop complaining, Ori. Don't upset the pit with your pseudo-ideological whining. Besides, class consciousness is a fairy tale no one believes in anymore – not even you. Workers like you have become part of the middle-class. They've taken all their worldly possessions and have made the pit their home – and they even like it down there."

"Good for them!"

The Boss slowly climbs down the ladder. He proceeds so slowly that the ladder swings in the semi-darkness of the pit, making him look more like a hanging prosciutto curing in a warehouse than a competent boss."

"Aren't you happy in the pit, Ori?"

"I don't know, I just got here. I'll have to see how it feels first."

"That's why we're here, my friend: to inspect, measure, test out and approve the pit. Any objections?"

"No... not yet."

"Good."

"But...."

"No! Don't even think about it.

"Forget I mentioned it, Boss."

Just a few centimeters from the bottom of the pit, the Boss lets go of the ladder and lands on the ground with a little jump, causing a small dust cloud to fall from above.

"Here I am, right next to you, you wretch. So, in a nutshell, this the bottom of the pit?"

"In a nutshell," Ori nods.

"In a nutshell, what? You some kind of a parrot?

"You can say 'a nutshell,' and I can't?"

"In a nutshell... no, you can't, absolutely not! Update me on situation, instead, you nitwit! Come on, spit it out!"

Ori's eyes widen. He doesn't know what to say.

"I told you to go ahead and check things out, right? It's not like I told you to go to hell.

"If you only knew how many times, though, I've told *you* to go to... right, Boss."

The Boss doesn't catch the jab.

"And what did you observe during your observation, you fool?"

Ori thinks about it for a moment. "What do you want me to say, other than it wasn't a good idea coming down into the pit"

"We had no choice," the Boss replies as justification. "Besides, it's not that bad down here. Don't you think?"

Ori looks around in vain, due to the pitch-black darkness of the pit. "I have no idea. I can't see a thing."

"What a shame. I would've like to have seen what the inside of a pit is made of."

"Take your time. While you're looking around, though, can I go back up into the open air?"

The Boss suspiciously looks at him. "What's the hurry? You have something to hide?"

"Who? Me?"

"You afraid I'm going to find out that you've excavated badly and too quickly?"

"Look, I dug the hole, it's right here, and it's all yours."

"But, how do you know it's here, if you just admitted that you can't see a thing!"

"There's no way to see where it ends, is what I meant. What more do you want me to say?"

"It's easy to pronounce the word hole. However, there is a hole, and there is a *hole*. For instance..." The Boss is stopped by a strange noise, as if the pit were human intestines in the midst of digesting something – or someone? Something is suspicious. "Hey, what's that noise? What does it mean?"

"I don't know, Boss. Maybe some kind of acid reflux," Ori hypothesizes.

"Acid reflux? C-c-coming fr-fr-from th-the pit?" the Boss stutters fearfully.

"Well, now you know why I didn't want to c-c-come d-down f-first," Ori purposely stutters, with a small smile of satisfaction on his face.

"Then, why did you make me come down second, right after you? Why didn't you warn me of the impending danger?"

"Because you're the Boss, so you too have to understand, or rather, be aware of what's happening in the pit."

"Ori, the pit is my responsibility when it comes to the orders, shifts and the turnover of personnel. However, the interior of the pit is your work, therefore – and a 'therefore' is necessary here – *therefore*, the responsibility for its construction falls squarely on you. If the pit were to suddenly collapse – let's knock as hard as possible on wood that it doesn't – who do think would be at fault? I, who have put my faith in you, or you, who have taken advantage of my unconditional trust?"

Ori, who is beyond speechless and dumbstruck by the Boss's fierce scrutiny, is irresponsibly indifferent as he lets out a surly, "Beats me!"

The Boss is utterly fed up with his attitude, which falls somewhere between revolutionary defeatism and atavistic indifference. "You cave-dwelling troglodyte! You're truly the picture-perfect image of this fucking pit. You, you… what's the word I'm thinking of? You two are made for each other! And, stopping taking advantage of the darkness to touch my ass!"

This time, Ori explicitly refuses to get personally involved and simply says, "It wasn't me, Boss."

"And whose tentacle was that, in your opinion, the pit's?"

"I don't know, Boss; I just know it wasn't mine. Maybe it's coming from an octopus lair… yeah, that's it, a sea monster."

"And where's the ocean, you idiot!?"

"How should I know, Boss; below us, maybe?"

"You dug this pit with your own hands, so if you don't know, how do expect me to. You should know it like inside of your pockets – even better!"

"I only contributed to the work. I couldn't have completed it on my own. My knowledge of the pit is limited to its very excavation. But a pit like this isn't created on a whim: there needs to be precise planning, a reason, a motive, which I can't know in all its complexity. All I did was to follow your orders to the letter. You told me to dig, and I dug."

"Well, at least now you have to realize that you went a little overboard! Sure, you executed the work conscientiously, I see that, for which you should receive praise. However… however, you jerked the shovel handle so much that you've finished ahead of schedule, causing trouble for me."

"I'm sorry." Ori apologizes, temporarily letting go of his blue-collar stubbornness and pride."

"Sorry, my ass! How is Pit Management going handle the problem of a ditch completed ahead of schedule?"

"When was the pit supposed to be finished, Boss?"

The Boss doesn't have a quick answer for Ori. He stalls for a moment, then says, "They never gave me a due-date. It might seem strange, but that's the way it is. Look, I'm not the head honcho, I'm only *your* boss – so I'm only the small head honcho above *you!*"

"I already a have a small head above me. It's the one on top of my shoulders."

"The one you have is a bonehead: it's as hard as a rock, and stubborn"

"That might be true, but at least I don't send others to give my orders." Ori admits.

"I do, though, because that's my job. I *have* to say: 'You there, go tell Ori to dig.' and "You, go tell him to stop…""

Ori always finds something to poke holes in; it's in his wretched nature of being a bonehead. As a result, he never gives up the chance to break someone's so-called *nuts* and replies, "Well, you really never sent anyone to tell me to stop. You forgot to do that, Boss. That's why I continued to dig, day and night, while even neglecting to fulfill my duties as a husband."

"Then it's all your fault, Ori, if the pit has transformed itself into a tentacled monster, and your wife has turned you into a cuckold by taking advantage of my own personal tentacle."

Ori bears it, just as he's tolerated everything his entire life: being cuckolded and paying bills, paying bills and being cuckolded. Even now he tries to swallow the bitter pill given to him, just as he has always done. He's endured things and swallowed bitter pills throughout it all. Take for example the appetizing sandwiches he brings from home that the Boss continues to swindle out of him with the excuse of wanting a simple taste.

"I thought I was doing a good job, and making a good impression on you… all so I could get a raise, Boss."

"You were successful at that, Ori, and how! It was a pleasure seeing you dig that way, and I said to myself: 'digging is in his blood.' But I just forgot you to tell you to stop, because I was way too busy entertaining your sweet better-half."

"So, I worked until my hands were cut and bleeding for nothing!"

"Those are just superficial grazes. Instead, you should consider what you've done to this pit – it's a complete insult to the Earth's crust."

"And you have no idea, Boss, how hard the Earth's crust is."

"The problem is that you were much too enthusiastic – instead of poking around a little at a time, like I did with your wife."

This time, Ori reacts with pride. "Poke around a little at a time? That almost brings me to tears, Boss."

"Let it be a lesson to you – if and when there is ever another pit to dig."

"Another pit? No, Boss, I've already done my part."

"You've done your part, but you were too zealous."

"Too zealous, Boss?"

"Don't take it personally!"

"Who's taking it personally! Something that insignificant – not at all! Calling me zealous is nothing," is Ori's sad *mea culpa*, despite the fact that the word is completely foreign to him.

"Ori, I'm happy you acknowledge your mistakes. Make amends and repent about being that which you are: useless to yourself and to the consumeristic society into which you were born."

"The only mistake I made is not digging a way out of this pit: a social loophole able to help and cushion my exit from this place!"

"Poor Ori, don't look for exits where there are none. There can't be any, because if there were, this would no longer be a pit, but a fun place, like an amusement park. Speaking of which, have you ever taken a ride on the *Tunnel of Horrors?*"

"Yes, with my wife, Boss. It's called marriage."

"To be frank, I understand your existential condition of a worker on the edge of an abyss, that is, on the pit's border of imminent unemployment, and all the consequences that come with it: lack of self-esteem, a sense of loss of identity, human and social isolation, a lack of sexual activity and the subsequent fear of losing your reproductive abilities...."

"Meaning?" Ori says, somewhat lost.

"Meaning your wife threatens to stop screwing you if you lose your job at the pit. So, in order to make the best out of a bad situation, be sure to keep your job as husband and father completely separate from the one as an incompetent worker. Don't mix your private life with your professional one; never combine the Sacre with the profane... Just don't do it, Ori!"

"It's tough for people to separate themselves from their own human misfortunes, because they're always psychologically affected and conditioned by their surroundings – and by their wives who are always ranting about every new utility bill."

"Well, for that matter, even the pit's walls are closing in on you, but you don't seem to take that too seriously. It's as if you feel immune to the danger of an imminent collapse."

"No one's safe from the pit, not even me. I realize that, Boss."

"You'd never know it," the Boss says, prodding him.

Ori decides to express his most hidden desire, as if he were wishing on a fleeting shooting star that has appeared above the pit's sliver of a crater through which they descended.

"I'd really like to be able to fill it back in. I'd work day and night for free, if you gave me, I won't say the order, but a little permission to do so. Its very existence offends my intelligence. I know what I'm saying is serious, but it's the simple truth."

The Boss looks at him inquisitively. "What are you talking about?"

"My intelligence… never mind, forget about it, Boss! You wouldn't understand," he says and sighs, coming to the bitter realization that his unrefined linguistic terms will never convince the man he is speaking to.

The Boss believes the time has come to clarify things. "You think I wouldn't understand, you scoundrel? Do you think I don't see what's in this pit – the fact that there's nothing at all in here? Do you think the very concept of the pit fulfills my human ambitions and professional aspirations? Of course you do, why wouldn't you! Do you think I'm satisfied? When I was young, I broke my ass to study and graduate from college with honors; raise a family; feed and give my kids a weekly allowance; educate them by enrolling them in school and sports; only to end up digging – or making you dig – a damn underground hole full of nothing? What great a goal! Oh no, my friend, that's not the case at all!"

"Tell me about it, Boss!"

"The abyss below one's feet opens very slowly. At first you see nothing but a starry sky, maybe some overhanging clouds every now and then, but nothing serious, you understand. Sooner or later, those clouds clear, and once the twinkling stars reappear, you reach for them again, though with greater strength, and you're thrust into a world of ideals, hopes, dreams and illusions! Yes, stupid and empty illusions, because all of a sudden you wake from your drunkenness, and where do find yourself? Well, an example is right in front of you: in a ditch, from which you can now only barely glimpse a small part of that sky you used to dream of in your youth. Take me, for example; I studied aerospace engineering and wanted to send rockets to the most faraway planets. Instead, look how low I've sunk... into your filthy pit.

For a moment, Ori doesn't know whether to feel a little compassion for the vacuous being in front of him, with his cap pulled over his forehead, like a paper mâché soldier; or if it wouldn't be better to burst out in wholehearted laughter.

"Is that a confession, Boss?"

The Boss moves close to Ori's ear, then makes a gesture by putting his finger in front of his mouth. "Shhh! Keep it quiet, Ori. I wasn't taking an official position, just getting some personal things off my chest that must absolutely stay *inter nos* – between *us*. Understand? This conversation never happened!"

"But I think the same way as you do."

"Then, do you understand why I cannot give neither the order nor the permission to fill in the pit? The pit is now a set and incontrovertible fact. I told you to dig it. You dug it. Now it exists. What's done is done, and no boss can undo it."

"And, you would be the boss in question?"

"Exactly, and you, the worker."

"Right, the one who always gets screwed – you know, for a change."

"You might enjoy it – who knows. What are you complaining about, anyway? You have every damn thing you need, what more do you want?"

"A counter-order, Boss. Just as you gave me the order to dig, you should now simply give me the order to fill it in. The order to fill instead of to dig, that's all, and I'll close it up. Then, when it's done, when the dust settles, I'll just dig another one, which will be better sized for our needs."

The Boss considers the proposal unacceptable. "Idiot! Why would I have you fill in something you've just dug up? And why would I have you dig up something you've just filled in?"

"But be we wouldn't be digging the same pit. Instead, we'd be digging a new one to fill in the old one. And, if someone were to ask you, 'Are you digging?' you could simply say – with your professional conscience as ease – 'Yes, we're digging – and how we're digging!'"

"And if they get into details by asking, 'What are you digging?' How am I supposed to answer, huh? That the first pit was excavated badly, and we're trying to correct things by digging another? No, Ori, let's think carefully before taking some irreversible action that could jeopardize a reputation built up over many years of an honest career. For now, the pit will remain how and where is it.

"Boss, if we don't make a definitive decision right now – that of filling in the pit – we might never be able to escape it. We'll fall deeper into its maze, deeper into the void, which, for the moment, is hidden by a bottom that only seems solid, but that could suddenly become a quagmire of mud and shit!"

"Then, let it. This stupid and worthless hole is worse than all those ditches that came before it. It's become a revolting pit, the profound meaning of which we can't even understand. But the fact things have worked out this way for you, Ori, is destiny. Unfortunately, the pit is in your blood. That's why you hate it so much, because it' been part of you from birth.

"In truth, my birth was the first and last time I was able to get out of something."

"I've always said, Ori; you are a true son of a gun!"

"Excuse me?"

"In your childhood subconscious, the pit represents the vaginal cavity through which you were born, and to which you now have an obvious desire to return. Be honest, Ori, tell me from the heart, am I right? Be sincere…"

"I'm just saying that the pit could have turned out better than it did, and that's why it should be filled in and dug up again."

"Dug up again! Why would you want to dig it again?"

"Because it's lacking a foundation."

"What do you know about foundations?"

"I know it's a complete disaster when they're lacking."

"Are you saying the pit is unsound?"

"Yes."

"But you dug it."

"I dug it, but I didn't lay a foundation."

"What are your work responsibilities? Answer, you fool."

"To dig," Ori confirms.

"And did you dig?"

"And how!"

"Now we'll really find out if and how you've burrowed, seeing as you're complaining about a hole that you yourself dug. Let's measure its size… after all, we came down here to inspect, check, measure and report."

"Report to who?" is the question Ori is compelled to ask his superior.

"Whoever's in charge up there," is the Boss's short reply.

"How do you expect to report to someone above, if no one pulls you up and out of here first?" is Ori's bold rebuttal.

"Congratulations, Ori, that's a good question. You might be just a worker, but you're not as stupid as you look."

"And?" Ori presses him.

The Boss smiles condescendingly. "And… getting back to what you were saying. Imagine laying a foundation in a bottomless pit, when, as the word implies, it can never have one! It's threatening, crumbling, dangerous, and always on the brink of swallowing up everything and everyone. Otherwise, you wouldn't call it a bottomless pit, but rather a hotel room, a restaurant, a club, or better yet, a pizzeria – in that case, it would be a place of enjoyment, and not of death and sufferance, which it truly seems to be."

"What a wonderful point of view," Ori sarcastically laments.

"To make sense of the pit is like looking for reason in your farts, Ori, which are nothing but thin air, just like all your rebellious worker complaints. You're never satisfied: 'the shovel is too short,' 'The wheel barrel is too heavy,' 'That brick is too crooked,' 'The wood is too wet,' and 'The pit is too always deep.'

"Yes, but at least *I* did the hard work by digging it."

The Boss doesn't acknowledge Ori's jab. His attention is swayed by the zipper on the worker's uniform.

"Stay still, Ori, don't move…"

Ori jumps. He's frightened. The Boss immediately stifles his worries. "Cut it out, Ori, it's nothing. I just need a small stake, and it looks like you are well equipped to act as one."

Ori doesn't trust him. "Why do you need to use *me*?"

"I have to measure the pit, and I need you to be a point of reference for me. You're scared shitless of everything."

"I have to be a point of reference for you? What an honor!" Ori is delighted. Deep down inside, though, he would prefer not to act as point of reference, but someone needs to do it; so he unzips his work uniform a bit and mimes taking out marking stake, then uses himself by standing in place – upright and at attention.

"How's this?"

The Boss doesn't reply. He's intent on measuring the pit, which has turned out to be much more difficult than it first seemed. "One, two, three – how many steps did I take?"

"Three. Happy, Boss?"

The Boss throws his arms in the air as a sign of helplessness. "My God, it's really huge, gigantic…I'm drenched in sweat, and I haven't even gotten half way! What's it even good for?"

"Now you're asking me? It's been forever that I've have been asking you to explain the nature and meaning of the pit.

"I only gave you the order. It was you, though, who did the actual digging. You have more direct experience with it than I do. That's why I'm asking you for answers. And, put yourself away, that is, the marker. I don't need you anymore. I give up on measuring such a crater."

"But I'm stumbling around in dark, too," Ori dolefully replies as he zips up his worker uniform.

But the Boss doesn't give up. "What? The higher ups might ask: 'how could you have dug this much, and given so many orders to dig, without knowing the reason or purpose for the pit, or even the nature of it? Have you become such fools that you continued to dig under these circumstances?'"

"I have a reason for digging: it's called a salary, Boss. But do you know your reason for giving me the order to dig?"

"The Boss feels the sting. "How am I supposed to know? Do you think I know the reason and meaning of the orders I have to give? No one tells me anything, Ori. The order is to dig, and that's precisely why I tell you to dig. An order that is unclear to you is the same for me. It's just that in executing the order, you're aware of its meaning, the end point, the goal – the reason why you were given the order in the first place. It's easy for you! You just live with it. You dig a black hole, and as you continue to burrow down, you understand all whys and wherefores. If nothing else, the pit, the hole, the ditch, or whatever you want to call it, is an unalienated product of your work, and it provides you with just enough to get by. It's different for me, because the pit isn't mine: I don't own the land above it, I don't own the empty space created by it, and, unlike you, I can't say I've grown spiritually because of it. It means nothing; it's obscure and foreign to me. It's just a stupid, empty pit without meaning, and if I weren't your boss, I'd just be someone else's boss, maybe someone who's working on... I don't know... building some rocket bound for Pluto."

"A choice planet, Boss," Ori says, approvingly.

"It's funny, but that's the first place that came to mind. Who knows why?" the Boss asks himself.

"Maybe because it starts with the same letter as pit, or maybe because where there's a pit, there always a mountain... and you were thinking of some mountain on the surface of Pluto!" Ori's trivial joke doesn't even elicit a smile from the Boss, who scrutinizes him with a pitying look.

"You're not funny. Your jokes are just stupid comments that make no sense."

Ori, however, has other arrows in his quiver. "And the pit make sense, in your opinion?"

"No, dammit, it doesn't! We've learned that!"

"So, what sense was there in digging it?"

"Then, why did you dig it?"

"Why did you tell me to dig it?"

"Why didn't you refuse to dig it? Because, you benefited: by digging it, you got paid, right?"

"And why didn't you refuse to give me the order to dig? Because it was convenient to keep me working while you cozied up to my wife, right?"

"I have no intention of taking your place, Ori, so don't worry."

All of a sudden, the unidentified voice is heard anew over the loudspeaker and shakes the inside of the pit for the umpteenth time: "JUMP TO IT!"

"That completely unclear order… again."

"Unless it's a just a call *to order*, Ori. I'm sure that's what it is. We need to get back to work."

"What work? What do I have to do?"

"You don't know what to do?"

"I don't. Do you know what you need me to do?"

"Whatever you want, Ori."

"You like giving orders, but you're bad at it. You never know what orders to give when it's time for you to exercise that authority you claim was given to you from above. And I'd like to know from how high up you get your authority – to boot!"

"Fact is, you're not able to understand on your own what needs to be done.

"I'm not paid to understand on my own. I'm here to follow orders."

"Right, and what exactly are you paid to do?"

"To dig."

"And are you digging?"

"No," Ori says defiantly as he throws the shovel to the ground as a sign of revolt. "The hell I'm going dig, you've cut off my salary."

"The same old song and dance. I get it. You want to be rehired. Then, come up with something better in exchange. At least pretend you're working. Otherwise, you're going to cause problems for me too: 'You could have kept an eye on him!' 'You should have realized the mess he was making!' I can already hear my superiors up there. The ones who are always ready to cut me from the staff."

"Everyone gets the boss they deserve."

"Quiet! Pick up that shovel and start digging an emergency exit."

"And where would you like it to lead?"

"To the other side of the pit. We'll eventually end up somewhere."

"We'll end up in Hell, Boss!"

"Shut up and dig. That's an order. Just as we entered from above, we should be able to exit from below."

Ori doesn't trust him. "Can I say something?"

"As long as it's not bullshit, Ori, we can't afford to have any more crap in here without a way out."

"I'm working hard, dammit! But, be honest, whose side are you really on, mine or the pit's?"

"You amaze me. What do you mean, whose side am I on? I'm slightly bipartisan."

"Excuse me?"

"I mean, I'm on both sides. I think you're somewhat right and I think the pit's somewhat right. You have to understand that the truth doesn't fall solely on one side. You complain that the pit is too deep, and the pit complains that you've just dug too much. Who knows if we can find a middle ground, where both of you are right. I probably seem like a vile opportunist to you, Ori, but I am just being wise: I speak poorly of you when I speak well of the pit, and I speak poorly of the pit when I speak well of you. I balance myself Ori, on the edge of the abyss – constantly in play! Come on, be good now and dig."

"I would dig, Boss, but…"

The Boss doesn't like his use of the conditional tense.

"But what?"

"We have company."

"Is that right?" the Boss says suspiciously.

"It feels threatening and monstruous, Boss."

"Maybe it's some inhabitant of the pit who's fed up with all your chatter."

"Whatever you say, but it's holding a police baton."

"That's not a baton, Ori. Can't you see it's a wand?"

"Maybe it wants to beat us with that wand."

"I doubt it, considering it's just some kind of magic wand."

"What does it need a magic wand for?"

"To make a miracle happen, Ori: the miracle of filling in the pit and succeeding where we've miserably failed."

"Boss, you need to have your eyes checked. That's a police baton, and it looks pretty hard too…"

"Ori, you shouldn't be seeing police batons where there are only magic wands."

Ori is quite skeptical. "I think an order is ready to come down, Boss."

"Poor Ori, you're even mixing up advice with orders?"

"No. It all starts with simple advice: first for making purchases, then things move on to advice from boards of directors, and finally ends up with orders from ministerial and war councils.

You know where things are heading? To hell, that's where!"

"You know, you're always the same old pessimist… and even a little defeatist, too," the Boss replies, criticizing Ori.

Ori, however, doesn't feel at all reassured by the exaggerated Olympian calm of his superior.

"Get down, Boss. Some stern *advice* is about to come from above."

"You mean an order, this time? And what order would that be?" The Boss tries to comprehend, sensing the gravity of Ori's dark premonitions.

"The order, Boss, is… is…"

He can't finish sentence in time, because a preemptory and deafening "JUMP TO IT!" obliterates the words coming out of his mouth, and the impact of its meaning sucks him into the labyrinth of the pit.

"Hey, was that *jump* or *slump*. I couldn't make it out. Where'd you go? Don't me leave alone, Ori. Was it *jump* or *slump*? Ori, what do we do? Should we *jump* or *slump*? I'm coming to find you, Ori, my friend. You even took your snack and cigarettes… what am I going to do without you?"

The Boss's voice becomes distant, and as it gets weaker and weaker, the echo of his words gets fainter and fainter. His words resound and overlap, like the wake of an ocean current that transforms itself into an indistinct frothy mass.

The reddened sphere of the full moon lights the opening of the pit, like a giant blood-red pupil looking through the microscope of existence. Under this immense lens, like bacteria searching for an organism to latch onto, two human larvae are stumbling through piles of refuse laying on the bottom the pit, which has grown to the dimensions of a metaphorical – though considerably less metaphorical at this point – garbage dump.

CHAPTER FOUR

Appendix: Keeping Time in the Pit.

The clock hanging in the Pit work zone has two enormous black hands, roman numerals, is shaped as round as a full moon, and it is almost always fixed at XII o'clock.

The Boss has said that "that thing," a euphemism for something obsolete (a scrap of metal, or something to that effect), is broken and Pit Management will see to fixing it – his exact words being: "soon rather than later."

"What does that mean?" is the query of the worker, who is fully conscious of the fact that his work life depends on a well-functioning time measuring instrument in the pit that indicates when to start digging and when to stop... etcetera, etcetera.

"It means, in due time, ignoramus."

In effect, the Boss's reply explains everything, and nothing at all... What does "in due time" really mean?

"We'll see," Ori dolefully concludes. He certainly can't call into question the schedule and priorities of the work zone, not having neither the authority nor the expertise to do so.

Ori is crouching behind a pile of mud and debris that has just been dug out of the Pit, and he's taking the last drag from a cigarette butt he has smoked down to the filter – enough to burn his yellow nicotine tinted fingers. As he hypnotically stares at the hands of the broken time piece swaying in the wind above his head, all of a sudden, and without warning, he notices that – holy Moses – the hands aren't completely still.

"They're moving, Boss, the hands are moving!" Ori jumps to his feet and shouts out, as if he's just spotted America from aboard one of the three famous Caravels.

In fact, the second hand is vibrating non-stop; it's tremoring, like the hands of someone who's nerves are completely shot. It seems to want to shift, jump, dislodge itself from its stalled position but is being influenced by some mysterious force that's holding it in place, completely blocking it. Yet, Ori, just like someone who can't seem to mind his or her own business, continues to stare, and his bulging eyes, those two ocular bulbs bursting from their spheres, perceive the hand's ever so slight will to move by *motu proprio*.

"It's an optical illusion," the Boss proclaims, "Don't waste your time with that broken-down clock."

But Ori knows how to counter, just as he's done in other cases, like when he comes up with excuses to justify his slacking off. "We're wasting a lot time because of that broken clock: everyone is thinking it's always noon, so no one's lunch break ever ends."

The Boss is amazed at Ori's ingenuity. "If that were the case, the company would have definitely fixed it, right? Of course they would have! So, what do you think that means? It means the clock isn't stopped at the noon, but at 11:59 – one minute *before* the longed-awaited lunch break. You can just sit there and wait in hope, but you're nothing more than idiot, boor, bungler, slob!" he replies, though he knows he could be even more severe in his language.

The insults infuriate and drive Ori mad. "What does Pit Management gain from screwing us out of a few minutes of rest between one shift and another?"

"You don't think management benefits from it? And what about principle?"

"What principle, dammit!?"

"The principle that in Italy we work one minute more compared to other European countries, because here the clocks are always broken."

"What does that mean?"

"What does that mean? You're always so inquisitive. It convinces foreign investors to invest in us."

"Are foreign investors such suckers that they would invest in a clock that doesn't work? In a Pit where we've hit bottom? With a Boss like you and..." Ori pauses for a moment and continues to stare at clock's hand, which seems held back by some titanic force, then he concludes, "... and a worker like me?"

"Right," the Boss affirms. "You're good for nothing, and I don't keep an eye on you as I should. But, from this time forward, things are going to change."

"From *what* time forward," brays Ori in all his helplessness, "if we don't even know exactly what the hell time it is right now?"

The worker is not completely wrong. Even the Boss is forced to nod and sigh. He doesn't want to give in, but he can't ignore the most evident of evidence. It's precisely at this juncture, in this brief span of suspended time, in which the Boss seems incapable of any solution, that Ori – just like the saint that was blinded on the way to Damascus – sees the light and comes up with an ingenious idea. His plan would be to use the shovel handle to tap the clock's second hand in order to make the jammed mechanism start ticking again. Without saying a word, Ori extends the tool toward the company clock and pokes the second hand with the handle – just as you would do to a snake, to avoid running the risk of a treacherous bite in the event the serpent is alive. However, instead of moving forward after being poked by Ori's shovel, the hand breaks off and falls, sticking in the ground like an arrow sent from Heaven. Ori is embarrassed, and the Boss justifiably shakes his head.

"You're a real klutz!" is his verdict. "You're worse than Cupid haphazardly shooting an arrow."

"You know, I've always said *half-assedly* and not *haphazardly*."

"You baboon. Is it possible you don't understand that if the clock is stopped at virtually the same moment as yesterday at this time, then it's destiny?

The categorically definitive statement, "then it's destiny," saddens Ori, who expresses all his discomfort with a childish: "Why?"

"It stopped long ago," the Boss explains, "which means it no longer indicates passing time, which, to the best of the Boss's recollection – that is, to the best of *my* recollection – is something it's never done in the first place. That means time technically continues to pass, but it's theoretically hindered by a clock that seems to be stopped at an abstractly fixed moment... are you following?"

"No, I'm not following at all."

In fact, Ori is initially lost in a mental void, his eyes bulging like two large eggs – again, sunny-side up. Then, however, he has a flash, a surge of pride, and he has his say. He is as frank as can be and doesn't beat around the bush.

"The fact is, the clock can't tick, because something is stopping it; maybe some dust from the work zone has gotten into the mechanism, and the wheels only need a simple cleaning."

"And you would like to be the one who gives the wheels that simple cleaning?"

"With your permission, Boss."

"My permission is not enough. You'll need official consent from Pit Management, which could refuse with the justification that only suited personnel can and must exclusively undertake such a technical enterprise."

"Shit! Would you mind translating what you just said?"

"What don't you understand?"

"What do you mean by *fluted* personnel?"

"Suited, Ori, suited personnel...."

"Stop quibbling and just answer: Who are these people with *flutes*...or... *suits*?"

Ori's question, as simple as it is, seems to make the Boss anxious, but he manages with a customary reply: "There's got to be someone in charge of work zone repairs – some asshole! Apologies to my superiors, but when it's necessary, it's necessary... we can't always hold our tongue, when something is due, it's due..."

"But how can they fix if everything tool here is broken: the shovel, the hoe, the spade, the pneumatic hammer, the electric drill, the *pull-stroke* saw..."

Ori stops short, realizing he's made a blunder that could have a double meaning; one that's fitting and one that's more subtle and nasty, almost... sexual in nature. Naturally, Ori had no intention of creating a linguistic double-entendre when randomly listing off the so-called *pull-stroke* saw, among the other tools of the trade. He wouldn't even be capable of doing so, for heaven's sake!

"I was obviously referring to the manual *semi-circular* saw and not the pulls and strokes you do in your office everyday..." he adds.

The worker's unsolicited explanation makes his superior initially burst out in thunderous laughter. Then, the Boss abruptly stops. Ori has managed to exceed the limits of the ridiculous by transforming nonsense into an explicit accusation regarding the seriousness of the work done by his direct and only superior.

"Because in your opinion, I'm only jerking around in my office, right?"

"Each one of us gets calluses in our own way, Boss! And you are a master when it comes to… calluses!" is Ori's immediate response.

It's difficult to describe the infuriated look that comes over the Boss's face – but let's give it a try all the same (besides, it's not going to make things any worse by putting it in writing): his right eyebrow rises to the border of his hairline, while the left one falls to the level of his lower lip; his mouth twists itself into a sneer, and from his clenched teeth, drool is dribbling down his chin. That very chin then wrinkles up like an elephant's skin, while his ears become so distorted by the twinging of his face, they take on the dimensions of the wings of a fire-breathing dragon. Ori semi-closes his eyes, and on the back of his neck, he feels the bumps of a goose that's just about to be swallowed up by an ogre. Nevertheless, the sensation passes in the blink of an eye, because, when it comes down to it, the worker knows that the Boss is harmless, powerless, not at all capable of reacting rashly. Anyhow, the worse he could do is to make the worker's life difficult in the Pit. Right, but how can you make someone's life even tougher in such a place as this? So, Ori responds by shrugging his shoulders, which, though it's not very respectful to someone in authority, produces the desired effect of calming the Boss's infuriated temperament, bringing it down to an appropriate milder tone.

"Are you shrugging your shoulders, Ori?"

"No, I was just shaking things off," he replies, minimizing the situation with the proletariat skill of someone who doesn't want to be caught in the act. "There's a big difference between shaking things off and shrugging your shoulders. Shaking things off means someone cares, while truly shrugging your shoulders is the same as a condescending sigh, or a simple way of saying, 'What the hell do I know?!'"

The Boss holds back his irritation and simply says, "You must be up all night thinking these things through, just like the all the other idiocies you spout out to try and convince me – uselessly, by the way – that you're not a complete dimwit. Well, don't be under the impression you've discovered the formula for soap bubbles. Know that the cultural gap between us has been and will continue to be IN – FI – NITE for a long a time to come… maybe forever!"

Having said this, the Boss stares at the clumsy worker, whose grey matter seems to be bubbling in its exertion to find a neuron to connect with the concept of *cultural GAP*. The

Boss believes he's defeated him with the simple sound of his big words. However, Ori doesn't give in. He rises up, fists on hips, which are as limp as foam rubber; the butt of a cigarette between the knuckles of his fingers; and his belt sticking out sideways, like some bodily appendage barely being held in by the work uniform. The malepeggio – a small chipping hammer used to dig into hard surfaces – which is hanging on his belt and easily accessible in case of emergency, stands to attention, like a living and pulsating piece of flesh.

The Boss bursts out in laughter after looking in disgust at the ridiculous position assumed by the worker, who wants to seem like a hard-ass – though the only thing hard about him is the erect malepeggio sticking out from his body like some strange protuberance.

"Give me a break!"

Ori, however, doesn't lose heart so easily, and, after not having been taken seriously, he follows the Boss as he walks away. The Boss stops when he feels the tip of the malepeggio handle poke him in the behind. Ori is proudly waving it as if it were a farmer's sickle during the Russian Revolution. Maybe the malepeggio and screwdriver will be the future symbols of communist ideology. Right now, they're both just considered work tools, with the screwdriver representing the current uncomfortable situation of the working class, in that it is indeed completely *screwed*! The tool and the term are both symbolic and deprecating.

The Boss justly reprimands Ori. "What the hell, Ori! Be careful with that malepeggio! If you think things are bad now, it's going to get a lot worse for you, if you touch me again in an inappropriate sexual manner!"

"Sorry, Boss." Ori takes a step back, not yet knowing he has created a new symbol of the Party, above and beyond the metaphorical sexual image to which the Boss alludes. However, he doesn't feel he should just give in and stop fighting, so he continues with his own form of dialectical protest.

"What it comes down to is this, Boss: you like using big words to make things tough for me to understand, to confuse and mislead me – just like those smartass political con artists, and all those financial sharks who gorge themselves on my pension fund by talking to me about investments and assuring me of pickup in the job market. Understand?"

"Mislead you? How am I misleading you, in your modest – and I emphasize 'modest' – opinion?"

"Mislead me from the fact that time continues to pass while the Pit's clock is at a standstill. Does that seem right to you? That puts us employees in a tough spot, because we never know how long we've been working and how much we've accomplished…"

The Boss cuts him off, because he feels that the ground he's standing on is becoming a slippery slope. "If you want to try and fix the clock, be my guest. However, considering I see it as a waste, you can do it on your own, without claiming overtime. It's useless for you to even try to claim the hours, because I won't authorize any extra pay..."

Having said that, the Boss goes into his shack situated on the edge of the Pit. Ori, on the other hand, is as still as stone, staring at the clock's minute hand, which is stuck in a heap of dirt, like a projectile fired from some alien spacecraft. A cold gust blows over the work zone, and it creates a purplish-blue dust cloud rising from the mounds of pozzolana used to reinforce surfaces.

Ori suddenly realizes that his inertia and lack of action are being caused by the immobile and paralytic timepiece: it is surely a type of psychophysiological influence that has his nerves all tensed up, and him on the brink of *jumping to it*, without his brain being able to initiate any movement. However, why should Ori's mind give his body an order to move and initiate anything at all? When it comes down to it, he has been absolutely forbidden to give orders to anyone, never mind to himself.

So, he gives the situation much thought and... *That's why the clock won't move!* Though Ori is literally at a standstill, he has a stroke of intuition all the same: he understands the tragic condition of the worker, who, though having a shovel in hand, can't move, because no one is giving the order to dig. Notwithstanding this, his awareness offers a glimmer of truth regarding the broken clock: it can't move, because it lacks its own interior will. And if it lacks will, because of some technical breakdown or mechanical accident, someone has to rectify the problem and give it the ability to regain impetus, momentum to move its hands and use them to finally advance time – and maybe history itself.

"It's time to move our ass, dammit," he says, fraternizing with the broken clock.

Naturally, the metaphor of frozen time, of history at a standstill and left in the lurch, is not at all original; literature is full of lofty examples that could be easily cited. However, let Ori deceive himself that he's capable of finding a solution, a remedy. Let him believe he's able to repair and restart the jammed mechanism, as if his fervor to be a fixer and reformer of broken things (and he's well aware there are a lot of like-minded individuals out there) were something that's truly new, unusual and unexpected. Does he really believe there have never been shakeups in the status quo, revolutions, fallen empires, or other pits that have never collapsed?

So, let Ori delude himself of being, if not truly useful, at least good for a little something. Besides, because of his worker naivety, the poor guy has no concept nor notion of so-called class struggle. *Struggle* and *social class* are words that no longer have meaning for the simple fact that the Pit now has only one employee: him – the last worker in history of the world. And, an isolated individual – even with a shovel in hand and ready to dig – can't start a revolution alone. Someone like that can't start anything at all and, just like Ori, is stuck. Completely screwed!

Of course, prior to becoming a hole without meaning, the Pit was destined to be something completely different – when the work zone was full of life, activity, with a significant work force intent on puncturing, drilling, piercing, riveting and digging; followed by stopping up the leaks and filling in the cracks resulting from the work. Now, however, there is a silence, as heavy as lead, weighing on this desertic and desolate place, where only Ori, the eternal worker, and his equally eternal Boss, remain.

They are polar opposites, magnetically positive and negative elements, though metaphorically attracted to each other.

However, what if he and that wretched boss of his are really only two faces of the same coin? Ori's reasoning is this: what if he and the Boss were the same person? It's likely that if Ori had realized this earlier in his work life, doors would have burst open on completely new worlds for him. He'd now be a captain on the bridge of a ship in a land of leisure and pleasant idleness. He wouldn't have to rack his brain trying to figure out what to do, because those who give orders, don't have to do anything at all, other than assume the responsibly and sleep soundly on it. Besides, no one is going to ask a boss to account for the orders that were, or were never, given. If he had been able to attain the ambitious position of boss, he would be strolling around the construction c zone with a cigarette in his mouth, warning, reprimanding, threatening, and, if necessary, immediately firing slackers and insubordinates, which make up almost the entire stinking work force.

Of course, he too would find himself facing the classic queries of whatever poor Ori is working at time – which in this case would be some completely different individual, another unfortunate and scorned worker, who would be able to question him up and down by asking, "Why would you want to fire nearly the entire work force on the spot. What reason would you have to do that?"

"In order to hire other workers to fire tomorrow or the next day, imbecile!" Ori would say, as Boss, to the other Ori, who would want to smack him in the face or, at the very least, spit in his eye.

That's right, dammit! How many times has Ori (the real one that we've grown to know up until now) wanted to smack the Boss's face. And how often has the Boss busted Ori's chops, contesting even his right to have a cigarette between one devasting work shift and another.

"Be careful," the Boss systematically reproaches when Ori feels the need to take a breather. "Be careful, because Management could decide to out-source the work in the Pit, and send it abroad. If they were to close down the Pit, it could even affect me, you know. So, put the cigarette out, stop thinking only about getting laid, and get back on the assembly line."

"There's only one line here!" Ori desperately brays like a mule who's finished eating the last strand of hay. "The one that was wrapped around my neck when I was born a worker, dammit, in a world that is no longer in need of manual laborers."

Ori's reflections on the labor market, the internal and external regulations of the work zone, thoughts on laws and dispositions, are all useless. The Boss knows well that the world isn't the place it should have been, but the place that it actually is. Period. Nevertheless, Ori has already decided that when it comes to the clock, it's time to intervene. So, he rushes into the tool shed, and in a flash, assembles a veritable arsenal of instruments for a top-of-the-line surgical intervention. In fact, he arms himself with a shovel and pneumatic hammer, a spade and hoe, a power drill and electric saw, a hand drill and ax, a nail gun and straight grinder, and he employs a rusty wheel barrel with a flat tire to move the everything. Then, he throws a wooden ladder over his shoulder, and teetering like a trackless tank, he transports the tools to a shady area under the timepiece. He then takes out an electrician's screwdriver, and he daringly ascends the rickety ladder. The rungs menacingly creak, as if they were barely supporting the massive frame of the worker, who takes much more pleasure in coiling spaghetti around a fork, than fastening screws, washers and bolts.

He reaches the clock, which is hanging like a stalactite at the top of the Pit work zone. As soon as he points the screw gun toward the head of the fastener securing the cover of the timepiece, the surviving hand, which seems worn out by the useless attempts to move out of its immobile state, clicks and shifts a few millimeters – hot damn!

"It's a miracle!" shouts Ori with a bounce that causes him to lose his balance on the top of ladder.

Both the ladder and worker, one coiled around the other, like the single entity of two lovers of ballroom dancing, dangerously start teetering – which might seem comical to someone looking in the from the outside. So, let's sum things up: Ori is straddling the ladder, which seems like some kind of extension of his hairy legs, and both, like a single monstruous being, a human giraffe, take a series of small steps, just like a clown on stilts who's been kicked in the shins by some little rascal. Right at that moment, the Boss, hearing the commotion, comes out of his shack. Realizing the moving danger that has been created by the worker hovering atop the ladder, he grabs the rungs and acts as ballast, stopping the fall of both the tool and the fool.

"Now what are you doing, you bonehead?"

"Nothing, Boss." Ori keeps his composure. "Just my job."

"Meaning?"

"I fixed the clock!" Ori says quickly and triumphantly from atop his makeshift rostrum.

"Congratulations! It's a shame, though, that instead moving ahead, like other clocks, this thing is going backward. How do you explain that?"

"Hmmm, that's strange!" Ori notices that the hand is not moving as it should – that is, clockwise. Instead, it's going counterclockwise and not keeping passing time, but time that has already passed.

"You're the one who put your hands on it, so if *you* don't know what happened, who does…!?"

"I put my hands on it… so to speak, Boss," Ori whines from atop his precarious podium.

The Boss agitates the ladder like he's trying to shake rotten worm-eaten fruit from a tree.

"In your opinion, you clock abuser and profaner of pits, was this ladder made for ascending or descending?"

Good question.

"It depends, Boss. If you're wavering on the top of it, like me at this moment, then it was made for descending, but if someone is where you are right now, then it's made for ascending."

"A clock, on the other hand, is only made to go forward and not backward... Any objections?"

"Let me come down, please. I'm getting dizzy. I'll start getting sea sick, too, if you continue to rock me like a sparrow on a branch in the middle of a storm."

"Do me a favor, Ori. Warn me when you're about to throw up. That way, I'll move."

"Does that mean you won't let me down until I..."

The Boss sadistically smiles, and sings "*until, until*" like the chorus of some old song.

Ori decides to take action. "When I get down, I'm going to take a good swing at you, and then we'll see..."

"Take a swing at me? How dare you?"

"Don't worry, I would *like* to smack you, but I can't. I don't want to be accused of fracturing your nose, and stirring up all the union negotiations that go along with it. If anything, I'll give the clock a good smack, to knock it into shape."

"You'll damage it even more. Stop, you scoundrel!"

That "Stop" comes too late! Ori has already raised his arm to carry out the decision, but before he can exert his unilateral act of force, the clock falls from the pin holding it in place and crashes to the ground, breaking into a thousand pieces. At the sight of the calamity, the Boss lets go of the ladder and runs his fingers through his hair. Left unsupported, Ori falls like a ripened pear, followed by the ladder that lands on both the Boss and his Worker, wedging their heads between its rungs.

"The Pit's clock!" the Boss continues to repeat, as if it belonged to him and he really gave a damn.

"It was already broken, Boss," Ori whimpers, shrugging off any responsibility.

"Pick up the pieces, and put them back together, one by one."

Ori gets up and attempts to look for the clock pieces; the Boss gets up and tries to go back to his shack – but their heads are still stuck between the rungs of the ladder that has the semblance of a collar. The rungs mutually cancel out the directional force of each of the two men, and almost strangle them to death, just before they fall to the ground – exhausted and out of breath.

THE PIT

A (Sur) Reality based Satire in Three Acts and a Finale

By Enrico Bernard

Translation by Marco Remo Zanelli

Characters:

Ori is a humble being, down to earth, but not without moments of humor and genius. He has a difficult time dealing with his existential condition. His attitude is full of the healthy cosmic pessimism of the lower classes, which take comfort in the fact that things could be much worse – much, much worse. His dream – for which he keeps abreast of facts, though in the process developing a purely superficial culture for himself – is to be capable of answering the questions of a television quiz show, with the goal of winning big, all as a means of freeing himself from the servile condition euphemistically defined as "work."

The Boss is equally refined and stiff at the same time, akin to a marionette that walks and talks on command. He's always unbalanced and on the brink of falling, as if he were standing on some uncertain or temporary reality. His power is limited to giving orders to Ori, but he uses his meager authority to purposely subject his subordinate to a whole series of little torments that he justifies with reasoning drawn from the work regulations manual, which he himself doesn't even fully understand.

ACT ONE

We see a pile of dirt center stage. There are a few signs that read "Construction in Progress." Hidden by the pile of dirt, someone is digging fervidly from inside a pit. All of a sudden, we hear a thud, like the shovel has hit something solid. We then hear a voice from below.

ORI (*Offstage*)**:** Hey, I've hit something hard!

(Ori's head emerges from the hole. He is wearing a mining helmet with a light shining on the front of it.)

ORI: Hey, hey, we've hit bottom, we've really hit bottom. (*He waits for a reply, but there is none.*) Did you hear me? We've accidentally hit bottom… the bottom, dammit! It's never happened before… and it had to happen to me! What a day… what a crappy day! (*He looks into the pit and talks to someone below.*) No one gives a rat's ass… Yes, yes, I've repeated over and over… I'll shoot off a signal flare, ok? Though, who knows if they'll even notice… (*He sticks a flare in ground, he lights the fuse, covers his ears, but nothing happens.*) No bang? No boom? What a shitty signal flare…!

(Enter the Boss.)

BOSS: What are you booming about, Ori? You furious with the flares?

ORI: (*Looking back into the pit.*) Here's the Boss, guys!

BOSS: Yeah, here's the Boss… so what?

ORI: It's happened, Boss.

BOSS: What, Ori?

ORI: We've accidently hit the damn bottom.

BOSS: The damn bottom? Damn you, Ori.

ORI: Don't be upset with me, Boss.

BOSS: Then who should I be upset with?

ORI: Well, in short, it's the pit's fault; it allowed us to hit bottom…

BOSS: The pit let you hit bottom, and you're wasting time with fireworks?

ORI: What do you mean fireworks? That's an emergency signal flare. It should make a "boom" to alert everyone, get it? Instead, the thing is a fucking nightmare…

BOSS: You're never going to solve anything by swearing.

ORI: Sorry, Boss. I meant to say the thing isn't acting like an ordinary functioning flare.

BOSS: Listen: I've been watching you for a while now, you know? And I don't like you, Ori. No, it's not that I don't like you, it's just that you can turn an *ordinary fucking flare*... Ahhh, see what you're making me say?!... You can turn an *ordinary functioning flare*, which should only be used for emergencies, into a show of pyrotechnics to entertain the public.

ORI: This is a real emergency, not a game!

BOSS: Aside from the fact of whether it's a real emergency, or if that's a real signal flare or not, it should have gone off... or don't you trust our emergency procedures?

ORI: Oh, no, I wasn't calling into question our proven and tested emergency measures, but...

BOSS: Ok, then, let's hear it: why was it necessary to call for help, Ori?

ORI: Why? Because we hit bottom, Boss.

BOSS: You already said that.

ORI: Take a look, Boss, and you'll see what a mess we have on our hands.

BOSS: (*Looking in the pit.*) Yeah, I see… nice situation we have here. Are you sure you've really hit bottom?

ORI: Oh, boy, it's hard as a rock. Listen… (*Shouting into the pit.*) Guys, let the Boss hear the bottom of the pit.

(*We hear three blows.*)

BOSS: It really does seem to be the bottom. But I'm not surprised… I mean, no more than usual. Dig, dig, dig, and we were bound to hit it, sooner or later.

ORI: That's exactly why we're here, though… to dig!

BOSS: But we can't go any further down, right?

ORI: Right. There's nowhere else to go. And when you hit bottom, it's nothing to celebrate. Now it's even going to be tough to climb back out, to boot.

BOSS: At least we can't fall any lower.

ORI: (*Pause*) As long as there's not a second bottom, Boss.

BOSS: Bull.

ORI: If you say so! Maybe you're right.

BOSS: Forget about that. Can you see anything down there?

ORI: It's pitch dark.

BOSS: Are you sure there are no cracks of light?

ORI: We would have noticed them. We wouldn't have missed a crack of light down there, no matter how small.

BOSS: If you had found one, you would've sealed it up immediately, right Ori?

ORI: Yes, Boss!

BOSS: Remember, there can be no cracks.

ORI: Yes, sir, Boss!

BOSS: Good. That's how I like you: obedient and disciplined.

ORI: Other orders, Boss?

BOSS: I don't know. Should I have more?

ORI: I would think so. A respected boss always has orders to give, especially in such a quagmire.

BOSS: What do you know about quagmires, halfwit!

ORI: Sometimes after it rains, certain areas can become quagmires, and I like walking on the soft, squishy ground… just like in the pit.

BOSS: Those areas are swamps.

ORI: And to think, I looked it up in a language dictionary.

BOSS: Be careful of bad dictionaries and languages. Quagmires are often and purposely deceiving – they appear different than they truly are: in short, they're contradictory. Especially in the darkness of the pit.

ORI: So, what do I do?

BOSS: Your job: Obey. Period.

ORI: Obey what?

BOSS: The orders, you imbecile!

ORI: What orders? Orders haven't come down from above for a while now!

BOSS: For the moment, the order is to maintain order. Then we'll see. As proverb goes:

everything in due time. Or, should I believe you're in a hurry for a change in order?

ORI: If it were me, Boss… do you know where I would have told the orders to go? To he…"

BOSS: Quiet!

ORI: I can't even curse?

BOSS: Why? Can you tell me what do you have to complain about?

ORI: A little bit about everything, Boss.

BOSS: Do you think complaining is good?

ORI: No, Boss, of course not.

BOSS: You see, I'm right.

ORI: You're always right, Boss. But…

BOSS: But what?

ORI: Once you hit bottom, you start to ask: "Now, what do we do? Sit here and do nothing?" No orders are coming down… and no one knows what to do… so then you ask yourself… "What if they never come down?… How long can we sit here twiddling our thumbs?"

BOSS: Enough! No *ifs, ands, OR buts*! The orders will get here. I can't assure you they'll be on time, but there's no doubt about the fact that they'll get here. Guaranteed!...

ORI: If you say so!

BOSS: You skeptical, Ori?

ORI: You know how it is! Any other time, I could've done without orders. When there was still digging to do, for example, we only heard one order: "dig, dig, dig." Now that we've hit bottom, though, and don't know if we'll have more to dig tomorrow, we need immediate orders, some certainty about our future, otherwise we are left at the mercy of only *rumors* that are unclear.

BOSS: You could've have obeyed when there was still more to dig, and therefore, orders to follow. Now that there are none, you want something to do. But it's too late. Now, you're screwed, Ori, so bend over and enjoy!

ORI: If there are no other orders, then there's no need for a boss!

BOSS: No need for me? Have you lost your mind? You damn well need me here!

ORI: Not at all.

BOSS: Hey, hey! Be careful!

ORI: There's no need for a boss when that boss has no more orders to give. Fact is, if you don't have orders to give, and nothing for me to obey, you are no longer my Boss. You're nothing – not even a good friend, and acquaintance, a neighbor. Nothing. Get it, Boss? You're absolutely nothing. Nil! Nada! Zippo! Zilch! A Zero Emeritus!

BOSS: If that's the way you feel, you're fired.

ORI: Oh, that's great! Why?

BOSS: For insubordination.

ORI: Insubor… what?

BOSS: It means refusing to follow orders.

ORI: No, it's *you* who's refusing to give them.

BOSS: You're right! The *order* is to not follow any orders, considering there are none. Ok? Happy now?

ORI: Oh, no! That answer is just a little too convenient for someone in your position.

BOSS: And it's just a little too convenient for someone in your position to obey orders only when you feel like it. That's not fair, Ori. You want things at the precise moment society doesn't have the luxury of being at your service to satisfy your every whim and clean up your every mess.

ORI: Is there at least someone above you who has the authority to give orders?

BOSS: I would hope so, by God! Now that you have, I mean, *we* have hit bottom – considering we're all in the same boat – I too am waiting for orders, in certain sense, and I find myself in the same embarrassing situation, believe me. Let's just try to get our act together. Ok, Ori?

ORI: Maybe you're right... (*He sits with his lunchbox on his lap. There's a pause.*) You believe in the orders, Boss?

BOSS: Some of your questions are stupid, Ori!

ORI: Well, maybe we shouldn't have hit bottom. Maybe we should've stopped sooner, that's all. At least, that's what I think.

BOSS: Did someone stick a shovel in your hand and say, "Work until you hit bottom?"

ORI: No.

BOSS: What was the order?

ORI: Dig, dig, dig.

BOSS: And did you dig?

ORI: And how! Feel these calluses! When I shake my pecker after taking a piss, it feels like it's rubbing up against two sheets of sandpaper!

BOSS: See? You so ineptly hit bottom out of either incompetence or extreme eagerness that you've stupidly developed sandpaper skin… or, rather, calluses on your hands. Can't you even admit that you overdid it, Ori?

ORI: If you make me dig like a mole without an order to stop, of course I'm going to hit bottom – sooner or later.

BOSS: And why did it happen *sooner* rather than *later*?

ORI: Because there wasn't any more ground under my feet, Boss.

BOSS: And you couldn't have noticed that in time – before it was gone?

ORI: I noticed it right when I hit bottom. When it was too late.

BOSS: You couldn't have just grazed the fu… frigging bottom?

ORI: Come on, Boss, don't look for excuses. It's not my fault that we've gotten to this point.

BOSS: It's not mine either.

ORI: Maybe not… (*He starts eating.*)

BOSS: What are you eating, Ori?

ORI: Just a little sandwich. Very, very little, Boss.

BOSS: Very little my ass! Is this any time for a lunch break, Ori?

ORI: It's noon, on the dot, Boss.

BOSS: My watch is slow. Luckily, my stomach is keeping time, Ori, otherwise, I would've given you a verbal warning. Instead, my stomach is warning you – hear it?

ORI: (*To himself*) Damn him! (*To the Boss*) You never bring your own food. (*Pause*) Would you like a bite, by chance?

BOSS: If you insist… just a bite; to taste it… (*He takes and shoves Ori's entire sandwich into his mouth.*).

ORI: You might have no orders, but you still have an appetite. Isn't that right, Boss?

BOSS: Always. Anyway, Ori, you should be thanking me. Don't you know that?

ORI: Really? Wow, you're such a great guy, Boss, I just didn't realize it.

BOSS: The sandwich wasn't that good. I've saved you the pain of having to eat it, so you didn't have to disappoint your wife. It had a strange aftertaste that I just can't pinpoint.

ORI: I can't say what the initial taste was like, because I wasn't even able to take a bite.

BOSS: I have to honestly say that the base taste of the sandwich was not bad at all. Next time you work the night shift, I'll go by your house and personally compliment your sweet wife. Any objections?

ORI: Then you'll get a good sense of aftertaste.

BOSS: And what a taste, I'm sure. (*He outlines the shape of a woman with his hands.*) Is there anything at all she wouldn't do for you! That's a statement, Ori, my friend, not a question. No offense.

ORI: Are you referring to something in particular?

BOSS: No, nothing at all, I was just joking around. (*He yawns.*) Now, leave me alone... Ah, well. (*He lies down.*) I don't think I could be any sleepier than I am!

ORI: What?! You have the nerve to take a nap?!

BOSS: So? What's wrong with that? If you were in my place, wouldn't you take a "moment to reflect?"

ORI: Maybe…

BOSS: Listen, Ori, this expression that comes out of your mouth every now is really getting on my nerves! What does that fu… frigging "maybe" mean?!

ORI: Don't get upset, Boss. If you say you're taking a "moment to reflect," I'm just saying that *maybe* you are. Period.

BOSS: In what sense… that *maybe* I'm not?!"

ORI: In my opinion, you're just killing time, because you have no orders to give, so there!

BOSS: I repeat for the umpteenth time: the order is to await orders. Understand?

ORI: So, we'll wait!

BOSS: *I'll* wait. You go down into the pit and get back to work. Any work. Now, get going!

ORI: Ok… (*He goes halfway into the pit, and we see him from the waste up.*)

BOSS: (*Pause*) Ori, what are you doing?

ORI: I have to take a piss, Boss.

BOSS: In the pit?

ORI: If not here, where?

BOSS: You're a troglodyte, Ori… Now I know where your nickname comes from: from *orina*, or so it's clear to you, urine! You make me sick!

ORI: Why? Hasn't there ever been a time when you couldn't hold it, Boss?

BOSS: Not in the pit, Ori! Not in the pit!

ORI: What's so special about the pit that we can't piss in it?

BOSS: Because it's *our* pit, don't you understand? Have a little respect, dammit! It might not be our cradle, but *maybe* our grave.

ORI: You too with the 'maybes,' huh, Boss?!

BOSS: I'm authorized to ponder such serious questions. Me, yes.

ORI: I piss on your questions.

BOSS: Ori, now I'm going to smash your face, because this isn't simple insubordination, but downright bad manners – not to mention you can't desecrate the pit and get away with it. Come on, put 'em up! (*He stands, puts his hands up and assumes a boxer's pose.*)

ORI: Hey, Boss, look what I found as I was urinating into your pit!

BOSS: Don't change the subject, Ori. Get up here and fight like a man.

ORI: You know how to use a typewriter, Boss?

BOSS: What's a typewriter have to do with anything?

ORI: (*Pulling a typewriter out of the pit.*) I found a typewriter. Maybe some journalist threw into the pit before moving on to TV news.

BOSS: Don't assume anything, Ori. You may even find a television in the pit, but that doesn't mean it'll be the end of civilization.

ORI: Or a refrigerator, Boss, but that doesn't mean it'll be full either.

BOSS Does it work?

ORI: Take a look. (*He hands him the typewriter.*)

BOSS: This thing is all wet. (*Pause*) Damn you, Ori!

ORI: Be patient. It'll dry.

BOSS: You're right, it really is a typewriter.

ORI: What's it good for?

BOSS: Idiot, it's right in the name: to *write*.

ORI: And to think, I pissed right on it.

BOSS: Inadvertently, I would hope.

ORI: I really needed to pee… not to write… never mind to read. I only read on the toilet, Boss, when I really have to go.

BOSS: You think like you dig, Ori: like a Neanderthal… you're pitting basic physiological needs against intellectual ones… you prefer toilet paper to the printed page…

ORI: Isn't hygiene a plus when it comes to our civilization?

BOSS: Civilization, dimwit, originated with the invention of writing, not toilet paper.

ORI: So, I found an archeological artifact. How much could it be worth?

BOSS: Don't get any ideas. This is property of Pit Management. (*Ori reaches for the typewriter.*) Hands off!

ORI: But *I* found it!

BOSS: Whatever is found in the pit, belongs to the pit. Stop complaining.

ORI: Damn pit!

BOSS: How dare you? It's given you work for so long; it's given you a typewriter to express yourself intellectually; and you have the gall to treat it like crap, and even piss in it?

ORI: Work has stalled, because the pit is done. And Pit Management has snatched up the typewriter, even though it's not *managing* a damn thing, considering no orders have come down. As for freedom of expression… we're better off just forgetting about that completely!

BOSS: Now I'm going to draft a few orders that'll your make hair stand on end, you moron!

ORI: What orders?

BOSS: I don't know… maybe the same ones as those that'll be coming down from the above.

ORI: And if they come by mail, I mean, already written?

BOSS: Then I'll rewrite them.

ORI: You're going to double your work?

BOSS: Even if they come down in person or by phone, someone from above will still have to write them up, because all orders have to appear in black and white. And I, who have a sense of duty, am going to put them in black in white beforehand. Any objections?

ORI: Don't orders ever come in color?

BOSS: You think too much, Ori.

ORI: And you work without thinking, Boss.

BOSS: Let's leave harsh judgements for future generations, Ori.

ORI: I doubt any of your written orders will be around for future generations… if you don't insert a sheet of paper first.

BOSS: Ha, ha, ha, that's true. I was typing without paper. Funny!

ORI: (*Surprised*) You mean, I'm right, Boss? That would be the first time you have – more or less unofficially – given me credit for being right.

BOSS: Don't be so surprised. My motto is, in fact, *render unto Caesar that which is Caesar's…* and unto Ori, that which is Ori's – naturally.

ORI: Thanks, Boss.

BOSS: That's my duty, Ori, my duty. Even if it can be so damn counter-productive to follow the rules so closely.

ORI: That sounds strange, coming from you.

BOSS: Think about it: if you had worked very, very slowly to buy time, there would still be a pit to finish. Would we have, or would we have not, both benefited from that?

ORI: If I didn't work fast, Boss, would you have, or would have not, fired me?

BOSS: If you only pretended to work fast, I would've only pretended to fire you. I would've laid you off, you would've collected unemployment benefits, then we would've started digging elsewhere, without being too obvious. One work zone here, another there… we would've made a good impression, gone through the motions and… voila! Instead…"

ORI: Instead?

BOSS: Instead, you took it too damn seriously. You turned a normal dig, a simple moving of dirt, into an endless pit that that puts us at risk of being buried under the weight of our mutual legal and, not to mention, po—li—ti—cal responsibilities.

ORI: I repeat: The order was to dig a pit, and I dug it.

BOSS: Then there's nothing left to do but to really fire you. I'm sorry, Ori.

ORI: If I can't collect unemployment, then you'll be digging my grave.

BOSS: Never give up, Ori… and good luck!

ORI: Don't you have a conscience?

BOSS: Ori, it's useless, it's all useless. The pit is done, and there are no other orders. I don't even know what's going to happen to me. Believe me when I say that I took action: I tried to create work, come up with orders on my own, but to no avail. So, there's nothing left but to pack it in… and look for other work.

ORI: What will you do?

BOSS: I'll stay here, on the front lines, and oversee the pit.

ORI: And if we were to fill it back in? Have you thought of that as a solution?

BOSS: We worked so hard to dig it up, and now you want to fill it in?

ORI: An open hole like that poses a danger: people could fall in and break their necks.

BOSS: That's true, too.

ORI: If someone gets hurt, the responsibility would fall on the work supervisor, Boss… meaning, *you*. You could run into problems, believe me, or worse: consequences that are more or less very serious.

BOSS: You're starting to make sense a little too often, Ori… at least for my taste.

ORI: You need to make a virtue of necessity, Boss.

BOSS: Of course, if I were in charge, I would take measures, or in this case, give other orders. But my role is limited. I can't bypass the chain of command. At least, I don't think so…

ORI: But that would be the most logical thing to do right now.

BOSS: Maybe those in charge are thinking the same thing as we are. I'll bet that's the case.

ORI: Not "maybe", Boss, they most certainly are.

BOSS: Yes, right… but I can't take on the responsibility, it's too great for me… Pre-empt the orders?… It's out of the question! If I only knew who were in charge, I could request an official and irrefutable written order!

ORI: So, what do you plan to do?

BOSS: We'll wait a little longer. Then we'll see. Only time will time will tell. Ok? Just to be clear, though, in the meantime, your salary is paused.

ORI: What can I say, Boss? Thank you!

BOSS: No problem. Don't lose heart. An order will come down in due time. Trust me.

ORI: As long it's not an order to fire me.

BOSS: You know, that would be pretty funny! A really good joke! Ha, ha, ha!

ORI: Well, I'd rather not think about it. You know what they say: if it ain't broken –

BOSS: – don't fix it! (*They sit on the edge of the pit. Ori lights a cigarette that he immediately passes to the Boss.*)

ORI: It's nice here, don't you think?

BOSS: It would be… if there weren't a pit with an unhealthy, stinking air emanating from its oozing putrid sewage… it's sickening!

ORI: Instead, I like the view *because* of the pit.

BOSS: I don't get you, Ori. I mean, I know you need the pit to carry on your wretched earthly existence – all that digging allows you to pay your oppressive monthly bills. But, you know, there's a big difference between that and thinking the pit is a perfect example of an ideal situation.

ORI: I know, but, unfortunately, that's a professional bias. I could almost say that I was born in the pit, and that's where I'll probably die. Though it gets deeper and deeper, it's still the same pit as that of my childhood: dark and distressing with no trace of light, a black hole, the bottom of a cave where you see shadows of an unreachable higher truth…

BOSS: It's unreachable for those who settle for less; for those, like you, who don't want to reach it, Ori. So, there it remains, at the bottom of that cave.

ORI: Boss, you know the orders better than I do: fill in any cracks of light, seal up any openings, hinder, hamper, obstruct any hope, and dig, dig, dig… I've never had any other choice.

BOSS: It's sad, Ori.

ORI: I'll admit that I've always had some hidden faith, though. I've often told myself: you'll see, the pit will be useful in building a solid infrastructure, a foundation for the future?

BOSS: I doubt it, Ori.

ORI: Me too, Boss. It was just a thought.

BOSS: A senseless thought. Listen and learn. I'm older and more experienced than you. I've seen many pits and few, very few, foundations. It's probably pessimism, but, unfortunately, that's just the way it is, Ori.

ORI: You're probably right, Boss.

BOSS: It is what it is, Ori.

(*The Boss continues to smoke. Ori wipes the sweat dripping down his face, he blows his nose, then dries a few fleeting tears. All of a sudden, the silence is broken by an imperious voice that is heard over the loudspeaker.*)

"JUMP TO IT!"

(*They both jump to their feet.*)

ORI: Did you hear that, Boss?

BOSS: You bet I did, Ori. It almost blew out my ear drums.

ORI: Could it have been an order?

BOSS: I don't know.

ORI: It seemed like an order to me.

BOSS: To me too, but I can't say for sure. If we obey it, and it's not an order, how will we look when one comes down that's official and by the book?

ORI: You don't know the difference, Boss?

BOSS: Between one order and another, yes, but knowing whether an order is official is much more difficult. Let me explain: In a certain sense, it's true that official orders are immediately identifiable, because they instruct you do something or not to do something. In short, what to do and what not to do, which, in theory, seems simple…

ORI: Ok.

BOSS: … but now, I have to admit that I'm a little unsure about what to do. Its meaning is unclear to me, provided it's even an order. The fact that it leaves you in a state of uncertainty means it might not be legitimate, at all.

ORI: Then what is it?

BOSS: That's the point. Yes, maybe it is an order, and it's telling us to "Jump to it!", so if we don't follow it, we're making a mistake. However, it's not a properly formatted order, and an order that's not officially clear can be justifiably ignored.

ORI: So, what do we do?

BOSS: Let me think.

ORI: (*After a pause.*) Excuse me, Boss, but what are the orders good for, anyway?

BOSS: To obey. An order is given for someone to follow.

ORI: That's logical.

BOSS: So, why are you asking me, if you already know?

ORI: It's just that there are way too many choices, Boss. One: to jump to it. Two: not to jump to it.

BOSS: I repeat, if the order were clear, we wouldn't have trouble choosing a side to take.

ORI: Left, or right?

BOSS: Those are driving directions. I'm talking about how to proceed, and that's where the first logical doubt comes into play. If we were to desert the center… of the pit, and leave it to the mercy of itself, you know what would happen? Instead of an order, we would have disorder. An order that directly results in disorder has to be balanced with an appropriate counter-order. Understand?

ORI: So, we shouldn't jump to it?

BOSS: No, we shouldn't jump to it. We can't jump to it, because if we do, we would be following the order, but we would also be disobeying the counter-order that's surely about to come down; there's no doubt that – you can bet your ass on it.

ORI: Are you sure?

BOSS: Trust me.

ORI: Ok, then, we won't make a move.

BOSS: No. We'll stay right here and wait for more precise orders. Anyway, that hideous ditch isn't going anywhere…

ORI: If you say so…

BOSS: Cigarette?

ORI: No thanks, I have my own.

BOSS: Exactly… give me one of yours, if you don't mind.

ORI: Not at all!

(They sit back down and smoke. All of a sudden, a multi-colored ball flies out of the pit.)

BOSS: Look, Ori, the pit has spit out a sphere.

ORI: Finally, something serious is happening! Now, we'll get somewhere… *(He bounces the ball, then throws back into the pit.)* Hole in one! *(He doesn't* *even have time to turn his back when the ball comes flying back out.*) The pit is in the game, Boss. (*He throws it back again.*) Hole in two!

BOSS: It just wants to distract you from your real problems, Ori. Don't get sucked in.

ORI: If it thinks throwing a ball around makes me happy, then it's making a big mistake. It would take a whole lot more for me to forget my state of affairs. Does it also think that watching a quiz show, a soap opera or a soccer match would ease my life's burden? Sure, it's better than a kick in the ass, but there's a huge difference between a distraction and completely forgetting one's true reality...

(*A raspberry sound is heard emanating from the pit.*)

"Phbbbbbbbbbbt"

BOSS: (*Referring to the raspberry sound.*) That's Karma, Ori. You treated the pit like a public restroom, now it's returning the favor by treating you like a fool!

ORI: Oh, really? Well, I have another arrow in my quiver! (*He starts to pull down his pants and squat over the pit.*) How about this, Boss?

BOSS: You're revolting, Ori. Give me another cigarette!

ORI: (*He pulls up his pants and looks in the cigarette pack.*) It's the last one, Boss.

BOSS: (*Takes the cigarette.*) That's one less you have to smoke. One day you'll thank me…

(*They sit back down and continue smoking. All of a sudden, we hear the voice again.*)

"JUMP TO IT!"

ORI: Should we jump to it now, Boss?!

BOSS: I've already said no, Ori! Please stop insisting.

ORI: It's not *me* that's insisting.

BOSS: God bless ignorance! I know it's not you who are insisting. But we've already established a course of action, and we can't go back on everything now just out of mental laziness or the simple fear of inconveniencing someone, dammit! We've agreed on the fact that the order has be clear and simple – without any obscurity or gray areas – for us to consider it bona fide, right?

ORI: Exactly right.

BOSS: Then, we can't jump to it after the second "jump to it," without explaining why we didn't jump to it after the first "jump to it," right?"

ORI: Right… because we didn't jump to it at all?

BOSS: Because there wasn't anything to jump to. At least, that's what we decided. We now have to stick to our understanding of things, if we don't want to seriously contradict our previous inaction, which we wouldn't be able to explain in any way, shape, or form. I don't know if I'm making myself clear, Ori.

ORI: More or less, Boss.

BOSS: That way, they'll learn not to send us orders that are unclear.

ORI: With all due respect, though, orders shouldn't be contested.

BOSS: So, you're already getting a big head? Have you forgotten that I'm the Boss around here? It's my job to decide which orders are valid and which are not; those that need further clarification, and those that are just blatantly inapplicable and counter-productive?

ORI: As long as you don't blame me for not wanting to jump to it.

BOSS: Did you jump to it? No, you didn't. So, what can I say? When it comes down to it, you didn't follow orders.

ORI: Right, because you *told* me not to.

BOSS: And, if *told* you to jump in a lake, would you have done that too?

ORI: Now I understand: you want to throw me off guard. You're going to jump to it, while telling me not to, so that I'm left looking like a slacker. But I'm not falling for it, Boss, because I'm going to jump to it before you do.

BOSS: Then I too am going to jump to it, buffoon.

(They position themselves like two sprinters. A waving red flag emerges from the pit.)

BOSS (*Stopping short.*) What's that, you wretch?!

ORI: Maybe it's false start signal.

BOSS: I'll tell you what it is: it's a red flag.

ORI: Red? It's only a little pink, Boss… a very vivid pink, I will admit, but… it's not red, no! A red flag wouldn't have been allowed to wave like that.

BOSS: On the contrary, it's redder than your brazen face. Now we really have hit bottom, Ori! It's shameful!

ORI: Maybe there are rough seas in the pit, and the harbormaster has raised a red flag to warn mariners of the high waves.

BOSS: Stop pulling my chain, Ori. That's not a red flag warning of rough seas, that's the red flag of the *Internationale*. Dammit – now I can unequivocally say that I'm infuriated as hell. And when I see red, I attack like the riot police…

ORI: (*Mimicking a bull fighter.*) Olé, Boss, olé.

BOSS: Stop joking around, Ori. We are in the grips of an historical anachronism, for which you are directly responsible. Admit it! (*He stops to catch his breath.*) You amaze me. I thought communism was dead and buried, and that the pit was its tomb.

ORI: Well, it's been regurgitated.

(*A black flag also appears from the pit.*)

BOSS: It looks like that sewer is regurgitating a little too much. See to it!

ORI: Right away, Boss. (*He goes halfway into the pit and is seen from the chest up.*)

BOSS: And tomorrow, bring two packs of cigarettes with you.

ORI: Two?

BOSS: One for you, and one for me.

ORI: Thanks for the tip. I won't forget.

BOSS: Good. (*He whistles for a short bit.*) Done? Come on, how long does it take you to bury communism, once and for all?

ORI: It's putting up a fight, Boss. Psychologically, it doesn't want to go underground. It's even trying to come to an agreement with the market economy.

BOSS: What a shitty pit!

ORI: And I'm in it up to my neck, Boss.

BOSS: You need to learn to adapt to the way things are, the way they've *jumped* into existence. It's already quite an undertaking to excavate a pit, but it's no concern of yours even if you were asked to dig a mine, an oil well or a grave. You earn your bread and butter by digging, digging and continuing to dig.

ORI: A grave, fine, that's fine, but I refuse to dig a cesspool, no way. I don't deserve that, dammit! I have upstanding years of seniority, and speaking of seniors, my grandfather was even part of the resistance.

BOSS: A partisan fighter?

ORI: No, a drunk. He was part of the resistance in the sense that he was arrested precisely for *resisting* arrest… and public disturbance. (*He puts one foot outside the pit.*)

BOSS: What are you doing? Who told to come out if the pit?

ORI: I'm done, Boss. So, if you don't mind, and more importantly, if you have no other orders…

BOSS: No, I have no other orders for the moment… (*He inspects the pit.*) Nice. Nice. Good job…

ORI: Satisfied, Boss? I buried it once and for all, right?

BOSS: You only did your duty, Ori. It's nothing that sensational. Don't get a big head over it.

ORI: Seeing as there are no other orders, and since you've *paused* my salary, I too want a pause from all the blood, sweat and tears I've put into my work… with your permission!

BOSS: Careful, Ori. The fact that I don't have any orders doesn't justify your indifference, your 'I don't give a crap attitude,' or your poor adherence to duty.

ORI: I hang onto whatever I can, Boss. As long as I don't' have to hang on to the tram when it's full, which is usually the case!

BOSS: I see you snickering under that mustache of yours, you bastard!

ORI: It's not a mustache, Boss, it's a grease mark; we work hard in that pit.

BOSS: It's doesn't look that way to me. Anyway, we'll see when the orders come down, Ori. If I were you, I'd be on edge. Who knows what they have in store for you.

ORI: What could they have me do? Dig another pit?

BOSS: Or another common grave! We'll see…

ORI: We'll see.

BOSS: *I* will see. You'll be down in the pit, working.

ORI: Working on what?

BOSS: I don't know at the moment, but I'll know before long.

ORI: To have a boss with no orders is the worst thing that can happen to someone who has better things to do in life.

BOSS: Why is that?

ORI: Because I have to obey, but I don't know what; and life goes on, but without anything concrete or positive about it.

BOSS: In meantime, obey *me*. That's your mission in life.

ORI: You're not an order, Boss.

BOSS: Be careful: you can't obey orders without a Boss.

ORI: And you can't obey a Boss without orders.

BOSS: What makes you so sure I really don't have any?

ORI: It seems clear to me: "If you had any, you would have given them."

BOSS: The problem is that you always have to nitpick.

ORI: The problem is that I'm right.

BOSS: Ok, ok, but tone it down. Tone it way down, understand? You are getting used to being "right" just a little too much. Know your place, understand. Sit! And don't piss me off… (*Ori sits like a dog.*) That's better, much better!

ORI: Woof! Woof!

BOSS: Have you lost your mind?

ORI: If I have to sit like a dog, I might well bark, too… Why don't you even throw me a bone?!

BOSS: Wait for the orders, for God' sake. If they tell you to act like a dog, you're completely authorized to act like a dog. You can even wag your tail and snap at people who grab it.

ORI: And lift my leg?

BOSS: Away from the pit, though.

ORI: Is that an order, Boss?

BOSS: Go fuck yourself, Ori.

ORI: You upset with me?

BOSS: You've gotten me into trouble, you idiot: "Hey, Boss, we've hit bottom, you have any other orders?" Where do expect me to get them, huh? Jackass! You've questioned my authority with your stupid attitude, and you've jeopardized my leadership. You shouldn't have done that, Ori, you shouldn't have asked me for orders that are just not coming down from above. I don't have any orders, understand? I don't have any! And I don't know how to get out of this tough situation – and I say "tough" only to downplay what it truly is: a really *shitty* situation. Can you understand how frustrating this is for me?

ORI: Poor Boss!

BOSS: I'm tired of being the boss, Ori.

ORI: You're tired of giving orders, and I'm tired of following them. So, we're even, Boss.

BOSS: Yes, we're even, Ori.

There's a brief pause, then we heard another thunderous:

"JUMP TO IT!"

ORI: Dammit, Boss, we shouldn't have let our guard down, we should've stayed alert. We should've known this was coming and prevented it.

BOSS: They let the bridle out a little, then all sudden they pull back on the reins with unimaginable force. Bastards!

ORI: Yeah! We don't even have time to enjoy a little healthy anarchy, a little homemade chaos, then all of a sudden from the disorder comes the order to "jump to it." Does that seem fair to you?

BOSS: No, Ori, it doesn't seem fair! This "jump to" it is getting on my nerves, and it's creepy too.

ORI: I'm not going to jump to it.

BOSS: Me neither.

(*The voice thunders even louder.*)

"JUMP TO IT!"

ORI: Hell! This time they really mean it, Boss!"

BOSS: You're right. It seems the those above us, way higher up, are making a great effort!

(*We hear the crack of a whip.*)

ORI: I'm scared, Boss.

BOSS*:* Jump to it, Ori, jump to it! (*He starts running but doesn't move. He then begins slowly moving backward toward the pit.*)

ORI: What are you doing, Boss? Why are you jumping to it in reverse?

BOSS: No, Ori, I'm trying to escape the pull coming from the pit, but I can't! It's amazing how many kilotons of energy a ditch like that can generate. We're heading straight for the ass of the hole, Ori, haven't you noticed?

ORI: Now I feel it. It's taken hold of me, too! I'm going to try to sprint ahead! (*He too begins to run, but also ends up moving backward toward the pit.*)

BOSS: It's like we're training for a new event: The 100-meter dash – IN REVERSE!

ORI: What you mean 100 meters? There are only a few centimeters left before we're completely swallowed up!

BOSS: Run, Ori, run!

ORI: Boss, don't hold onto me… you're going to tear my clothes off!

BOSS: You won't need clothes underground, Ori!

ORI: Oh, wow, the soles of my shoes have completely worn out, and my feet are now starting to cause friction on the ground! It burns!

BOSS: Ori, help!

ORI: We're falling, Boss! It's not right, but that's what's happening!

BOSS: What the fuck, Ori! Didn't you say that once you hit bottom, you can't sink any lower?!

ORI: Me?!

BOSS: Yes, you… it was you. I remember it perfectly!

ORI: Maybe I did, I say a lot of things!

BOSS: You imbecile! If I had really known the true state of things, I would've given some order to fix the problem. Who knows, maybe I would've had a mattress placed on the bottom – to soften the landing!

ORI: We're wavering, Boss!

BOSS: You go first! (*The Boss pushes Ori into the pit.*)

ORI: Ahhh! (*He disappears into the ditch.*)

BOSS: (*To himself*) That'll teach him not to dig holes big enough to fall into. (*Ori's hand emerges from the pit, grabs the Boss's ankle, and causes him to fall in too.*) Ahhh!

There is no one on stage for a moment, then a figure enters stage left dressed with a sandwich board that reads:

WE HEAR THE SOUND OF

Another figure enters stage right with a sandwich board that reads:

SNORING?

(*We hear snoring.*)

The stage left sign shakes its head: No! The stage right sign changes to:

COUGHING?

(*We hear coughing.*)

The stage left sign shakes its head: No! The stage right sign changes to:

A GUNSHOT?

(*We hear a gunshot.*)

The stage left sign grows impatient and changes its sign to read:

THERE'S A

The stage right sign changes to:

SCENE CHANGE?

The stage left sign grows even more impatient. The stage right sign changes for the last time to:

REGIME CHANGE!

(We hear the sounds of machine gun fire. The stage left sign smiles.)

BLACKOUT

Upstage, a sign illuminates, and it reads:

WE ARE EXPERIENCING TECHNICAL DIFFULTIES WITH OUR GLOBAL SATELLITE LINK

THE SHOW WILL RESUME AS SOON AS POSSIBLE

THANK YOU FOR YOUR PATIENCE

LIGHTS FADE UP

(Following a brief pause, we hear far-off sounds coming from the pit. They continue to get louder and clearer as an indication that work has resumed.)

BOSS: *(Offstage, from inside the pit.)* Hey! I I've hit something hard!

(The Boss's head emerges from the hole. He is wearing a mining helmet with a light shining on the front of it.)

Hey, hey, we've hit bottom, we've really hit bottom. *(He waits for a reply, but there is none.)* Did you hear me? We've accidently hit bottom… the bottom, dammit! It's never happened before… and it had to happen to me! What a day… what a crappy day! *(He looks into the pit and talks to someone below.)* No one gives a rat's ass… Yes, yes, I've repeated over and over… I'll shoot off a signal flare, ok? Though, who knows if they'll even notice… *(He sticks a flare in ground, he lights the fuse, covers his ears, but nothing happens.)* No bang? No boom? What a shitty signal flare…!

(Enter Ori)

ORI: What are you booming about, Boss? You furious with the flares?

BOSS: (*Looking back into the pit.*) Here's Ori, guys!

ORI: Yeah, here's Ori… so what?

BOSS: It's happened, Ori.

ORI: What, Boss?

BOSS: We've accidently hit the damn bottom.

ORI: The damn bottom? Damn you, Boss.

BOSS: Don't be upset with me, Ori.

ORI: Then, who should I be upset with?

BOSS: Well, in short, it's the pit's fault; it allowed us to hit bottom…

ORI: The pit let you hit bottom, and you're wasting time with fireworks?

BOSS: What do you mean fireworks? That's an emergency signal flare. It should make a "boom" to alert everyone, get it? Instead, the thing is a fucking nightmare…

ORI: You're never going to solve anything by swearing.

BOSS: Sorry, Ori. I meant to say the thing isn't acting like a ordinary functioning flare.

ORI: Listen: I've been watching you for a while now, you know? And I don't like you, Boss. No, it's not that I don't like you, it's just that you can turn an *ordinary fucking flare*... Ahhh, see what you're making me say?!... You can turn an *ordinary functioning flare*, which should only be used for emergencies, into a show of pyrotechnics to entertain the public.

BOSS: This is a real emergency, not a game!

ORI: Aside from the fact of whether it's a real emergency, or if that's a real signal flare or not, it should have gone off... or don't you trust our emergency procedures?

BOSS: Oh, no, I wasn't calling into question our proven and tested emergency measures, but...

ORI: Ok, then, let's hear it: why was it necessary to call for help, Boss?

BOSS: Why? Because we hit bottom, Ori.

ORI: You already said that.

BOSS: Look into the pit, Ori. You'll see what mess we have on our hands.

ORI: (*Looking into the pit.*) Yeah, I see... nice situation we have here. Are you sure you've really the bottom?

BOSS: Oh, boy, it's hard as a rock. Listen... (*Shouting into the pit.*) Guys, let Ori hear the bottom of the pit.

(*We hear three blows.*)

ORI: It really does seem to be the bottom. But I'm not surprised... I mean, no more surprised than usual. Dig, dig, dig, and we were bound to hit it, sooner or later.

BOSS: That's exactly why we're here, though... to dig!

ORI: We can't go any further down, right?

BOSS: Right. There's nowhere else to go. And when you hit bottom, it's nothing to celebrate. Now it's even going to be tough to climb back out, to boot.

ORI: At least we can't fall any lower.

BOSS: (*Pause*) As long as there's not a second bottom, Ori.

ORI: Bull.

BOSS: If you say so! Maybe you're right.

ORI: Forget about that. Can you see anything down there?
BOSS: It's pitch dark.

ORI: Are you sure there are no cracks of light?

BOSS: We would have noticed them. We wouldn't have missed a crack of light down there, no matter how small.

ORI: If you had found one, you would've sealed it up immediately, right Boss?

BOSS: Yes, Ori!

ORI: Remember, there can be no cracks.

BOSS: Yes, sir, Ori!

ORI: Good. That's how I like you: obedient and disciplined.

BOSS: Other orders, Ori?

(*An enormous shadow appears behind them.*)

ORI: I don't know. Should I have more?

BOSS: How should I know… you're in charge now, Ori.

ORI: "You're in charge now" is easier said than done.

BOSS: You're telling me?!

ORI: Hmm... who or what is that scarecrow looking thing?

BOSS: I've never seen it before in my life.

ORI: It looks threatening.

BOSS: Really?

ORI: It can't have good intentions with a police baton in hand

BOSS: Ori, that's not a police baton, you idiot. Can't you see it's a wand?

ORI: Maybe it wants to beat us with that wand.

BOSS: I doubt it, considering it's just some kind of magic wand.

ORI: And what does it need a magic wand for?

BOSS: To make a miracle happen, Ori: the miracle of filling the pit and succeeding where we've miserably failed.

ORI: Boss, you need to have your eyes checked. That's a police baton, and it looks pretty hard too…

BOSS: Ori, you're so stupid, you always see police batons where there are only magic wands.

ORI: I think an order is ready to come down, Boss.

BOSS: Poor Ori, you're even mixing up advice with orders.

ORI: No. It all starts with simple advice: first for making purchases, then it moves on to advice from boards of directors, and it ends up with orders from ministerial and war councils. You know where things are heading? To hell, that's where!

BOSS: You know, you're always the same old pessimist… and even a little bit defeatist, too.

ORI: Get down, Boss. Some stern *advice* is about to come from above.

BOSS: Do you mean an order, this time? And what order would that be?

(*The voice booms again, the sound shattering the stage.*)

"JUMP TO IT!"

(*Ori jumps into the pit*)

BOSS: Hey, was that *jump* or *slump*. I couldn't make it out. Where did you go, Ori? Don't leave me leave alone. Did the force of that *advice* push you into the pit? Come on, Ori, was is *jump* or *slump*? Ori, what do we do? Should we *jump* or *slump*? I coming to find you, Ori, my friend.

(*The Boss slowly descends into the pit, which gradually transforms itself into an infernal volcano that begins to erupt.*)

(END OF ACT ONE)

CURTAIN

ACT TWO

(Ori digs one last pile of dirt with a spade, then he wipes the sweat off his face with a colored handkerchief, which he also uses to blow his nose, just before utilizing again to wipe his forehead. He then slowly sits down and pulls out a pack of cigarettes.)

ORI: Well, we've made our bed, now we have to lie in it. *(Ori starts to light a cigarette. The Boss appears. He's frowning.)*

BOSS: What's going on here?

ORI: Nothing, Boss.

BOSS: What do you mean nothing?

ORI: Nothing's going on, Boss.

BOSS: Exactly, Ori, I can see that. You are doing precisely nothing, A.K.A., you're taking it easy.

ORI: A.K.A.?

BOSS: It's a union term, slacker.

ORI: I'm just opposed to an A.K.A., that's all – whatever it is.

BOSS: And I'm opposed to smoke.

ORI: Even outside?

BOSS: I don't give a damn if it's outside; not while you're on the clock!

ORI: It's just a short cigarette-break, Boss.

BOSS: A cigarette-break? You've already taken a cappuccino-break, a snack-break, a lunch-break, a coffee-break, an after-coffee-espresso-chaser-break. So, there is no cigarette-break.

ORI: I'm going to take one anyway.

BOSS: Then, you're going to skip the general work-break, right?

ORI: Right, I'll skip that… because, there's no more work left to do, anyway.

BOSS: What are you saying, Ori?

ORI: I'm saying that I've just finished digging the pit: look at that hole.

BOSS: Finished?

ORI: Fi – nish – ed.

BOSS: You're so naïve, Ori.

ORI: Why's that, Boss?

BOSS: Because you never finish digging a pit — the more you dig, the closer it gets to becoming what it really should be: deep.

ORI: Well, I've finished it!

BOSS: When?

ORI: A little while ago.

BOSS: And you couldn't have warned me?

ORI: I was going to, once I was done with my cigarette.

BOSS: So, on your list of priorities, I come after your cigarette-break?

ORI: Even after my coffee-break, for that matter.

BOSS: Skip it, dammit. What do you say we go down and have a look… to be sure it's really finished?

ORI: If you insist. Be my guest."

BOSS: You first, Ori, I'll be right behind…

ORI: No. Forget about being "right behind." You think I'm nuts?!

BOSS: Stop contradicting me. You know it's not worth it. Go down into the pit. That's an order, and when I give an order, you have to follow it, whether you like it or not – immediately: meaning, right away, on the spot, on your two feet, and without batting an eye. Understand?

ORI: You go first, Boss… please, be my guest.

BOSS: Why should I go first?

ORI: Because you come before me. Doesn't boss mean 'he who's first in line?' So, according to the definition…

BOSS: He who's first in line isn't the one who goes into the pit first. Look up the term! The way things are set down in the regulations, and in your work contract, is that Ori always goes in first…

ORI: And no doubt comes up last.

BOSS: Correct. See, you're not that stupid. Now you can understand what it means to be the boss. It's exhausting, believe me.

ORI: I can imagine. I only know what it's like being Ori, dammit!

BOSS: Really? And what does it mean to be Ori, in your opinion. Come on! Enlighten me! Surprise me with something intelligent that explains who you are and why you're working in this pit – if you're able to.

ORI: Ori comes from Orestes, Boss. I'll bet you didn't know that.

BOSS: You sure it doesn't come from *orina*, you know, urine?

ORI: No, Boss, Ori comes from Orestes not… *orina*. I'm sure about that, for heaven's sake!

BOSS: Funny. From the stink, I wouldn't have thought so… you smell like a latrine, Ori. How long do you stay in the company bathroom doing your business, huh?

ORI: Just enough time to read in *Trivia Weekly* that Orestes is Agamemnon and Clytemnestra's last-born child – and I made a mental note of it, too, in case someone calls from a television quiz show asking the question…

BOSS: You don't say! So, that's what public bathrooms are good for: to educate people like you who dream of solving their daily dramas by participating in some frivolous game show. I pity you, Ori, Orestes, Orina, or whatever you want to call yourself.

ORI: Ori only comes from Orestes, Boss, the brother of Electra.

BOSS: Then, you should have been an electrician, Ori, and not a general laborer. Truth is, one never knows what ask from a type like you: Electricity? Water? Gas? Masonry? Gardening?... No, you're only good for digging ditches. That's the bitter reality of your useless existential condition.

ORI: Excuse me, Boss, but what do you mean by "existential condition?"

BOSS: I'm talking about your life, stupid. Don't you understand that?

ORI: What's so interesting about my life that you have to always stick your nose in it?

BOSS: Nothing, that's just it. But there is one thing about you that I just can't bear.

ORI: That I refuse to go down into the pit first.

BOSS: That too. But I was referring to was your professional unreliability.

ORI: Meaning?

BOSS: Meaning you're a jack of all trades and a master of none. In short, you get along in life the way you do at work. You're a disaster! A catastrophe! A mess!

ORI: Who, me?

BOSS: Yes, you, Ori. You pick up things here and there, in a disorganized way, in the hopes of using them to answer correctly on some million-dollar quiz show, or to be capable of solving some complicated technical problem with the simple tap of a hammer. That, however, jeopardizes your work output. That's right, because if you're good with a shovel, you're always better with a hoe. And if you're good with a hoe, you're always better with a shovel. And, if you make the terrible decision of using a useless screwdriver to make an urgent repair, you'll find yourself unsurpassed in the ability to use a hacksaw. You dig ditches, but unfortunately, you're a complete failure. So, you might as well resign yourself to the facts and forget about Orestes…which doesn't suit you… and your sister Orina…

ORI: Electra! Zeus transformed her into a comet after the fall of Troy…

BOSS: The Fall of Troy! Ha, that's a fitting city for your sister, because she's so easy, she'll sleep with the first man she sees, just like Helen did. I wouldn't expect anything less from her.

ORI: But, Boss…

BOSS: No *buts*! Just get it into your head that you're going into the pit first – that same pit you just finished digging with such excessive determination. I hate even thinking about it!

ORI: Excessive determination?

BOSS: Shame on you, Ori. You not supposed to work that way. When all is said and done, you have to think about each of our vested interests: yours, which is to dig, and mine, which is to give you the order to dig. It's embarrassing to have to constantly watch your back and cover your ass, so I don't end up with my face flat on the ground, because of your human and artisanal stupidity! How do you think I'm going to look in the eyes of Management with you digging a pit like that – when only a little hole in the asphalt was necessary to lay two simple sewer pipes. We're talking about a sewer, Ori, Orestes, Orina – or whatever you want to be called – and not an underground temple to one of your occult gods.

ORI: Amen!

BOSS: Go, go in peace… right into the pit. I've preached enough for now. (*Pause*) What's wrong, Ori? Haven't you had enough? Why are looking at me like a living and breathing question mark? My God, you're a hard nut to crack; even harder than the bottom of the pit.

ORI: Can I say one thing, Boss?"

BOSS: Provided it's just one, Ori.

ORI: The trait of any self-respecting Boss is that of setting a good example, at least until that theory has been proven wrong.

BOSS: What are you trying to say?

ORI: Are you sure you're a self-respecting Boss?

BOSS: What kind of question is that!? Of course I am!

ORI: Then, set a good example, as laid out by the unwritten norms of common sense.

BOSS: How?

ORI: Simple: by going into the pit first.

BOSS: So, according to you, that would be "setting a good example?"

ORI: Oh, yes.

BOSS: Poor, Ori, you're so naïve. Things are not as simple as you think. You see, my friend, it's not me who's holding back. I'd be willing to go first, just to show you I'm not afraid of the dark, if nothing else. What's stopping me is the awareness that I am indispensable, being the person you directly report to. You understand? I'm not going in first, for your own good. You should thank me. Unfortunately, though, there's no gratitude in your heart, which is as hard as stone… So, after you, Ori…

ORI: Don't worry. If one boss were to croak, we could easily find another. So, please go ahead, be my guest… No need to worry about me. If anything happens, I'll easily manage without a boss, at least temporarily. Anyway, the only order you've been able to give up until now has become beyond monotonous: dig, dig, dig… and dig some more. You didn't even realize we were about to hit bottom!

BOSS: I accept your challenge. But, think about it for a minute: just as a Boss like me can be replaced, a ditch digger like you can be substituted all the more so. As you can see, your stubbornness has led us down a dead end. Happy now?

ORI: What do you mean?

BOSS: An interruption in work on the edge of the pit is as pathetic as it is dangerous, Ori. The ground under our feet could cave in without a moment's notice. And then who would be to blame. I don't know about you, but I'd be forced blame someone by the name of Ori

ORI: And why is that?

BOSS: Because it's my responsibility to inspect the pit, while it's your explicit duty to give me the all-clear to do so – whether you like it or not!

ORI: Can't we at least flip to decide who goes in first?

BOSS: Not on your life. I have no intention of entrusting my decisions to whims of fate, Ori, and certainly not to a game of chance. Besides, you dug it, so if you don't want to go in first, it means you don't trust your own work. Did you follow my directives, Ori?

ORI: Of course I did.

BOSS: You didn't create some strange mess down there, did you?

ORI: Me, create a strange mess? No one gave me that order.

BOSS: Good. Then show me the faith you have in your work by checking things out first.

ORI: No, no, no. I'm afraid of the unknown, Boss.

BOSS: I doubt you dug so deep as to reach the unknown; at least I hope not. So, get down into the pit, right now! I repeat, that's an order — and not some suggestion from a friend who's telling you to take a vacation just so he can have some fun with your wife while you're gone.

ORI: What's my wife got to do with anything, Boss?

BOSS: Oh, she's involved, all right! I'm not suggesting you act like some Greek god, you know, like your namesake there. That would be asking too much. I'm not even saying to play a man that you're not. I'm only asking you to be the good worker that goes home to his wife every night — who in meantime is spending her days with someone else — only to receive a little kiss on your forehead and the leftovers from lunch.

ORI: Those are just theories based on nothing. At night, in fact, I don't eat leftovers, I cook instead.

BOSS: Show some balls, Ori, otherwise you're fucked! I'll fire you, and your wife will stop offering you the leftovers — and you know exactly what *leftovers* I'm talking about!

ORI: Damn pit!

BOSS: Stop making such a fuss, Ori. From the beginning of time, the chain of command has

always issued orders. The boss gives those orders
and simple workers like you–

ORI: –constantly get screwed.

BOSS: See? You know the old refrain. Maybe
you'll like getting screwed; you never know who's
doing the screwing. What does your wife say
about it, huh? Well, we know she takes what she
can get, and enjoys it. Ha, ha, ha!

(*Ori looks into the pit then backs away in horror.*)

ORI: Damn this world!

BOSS: Why are you blaming the world. It hasn't
done anything to you that's really bad or painful
– yet.

ORI: Yet? That's comforting… Who knows
what the world has in store for me, to finish off
its work of destroying a human being. It's been
ruthless to me all my life. Never a glimmer of
hope, a flicker of a bright future. You know what
tomorrow holds for me?

BOSS: I can only imagine; a payment installment
that's past due?

ORI: Or some other bill.

BOSS: How trivial.

ORI: The trick would be to be able to pay them on time, but I'm always past due, dammit!

BOSS: Stop whining. All things considered, no one has yet tried to completely destroy your existence. The world is only giving you as initial, small taste of its wickedness. It's only grazing you; the real bombardment is still waiting to hit you on the head.

ORI: I'm not whining, I'm just cursing the day I was born.

BOSS: You should have thought of that sooner. Now it's too late.

ORI: I know that, unfortunately. Well, I guess I have to be the one who goes in first.

BOSS: Finally, we have come to a decision.

ORI: We, Boss? You're using the plural?

BOSS: Don't get too attached to the subtleties of syntax, Ori, which wouldn't be able to support the not so trivial weight of your gross stupidity. Instead, make sure you secure yourself to ladder's ropes. I wouldn't want you to get hurt while descending, Ori, because then, you see, I'd have to make you utter the words: "mea culpa, mea culpa, mea maxima culpa." Go on, Ori, go ahead. You have my corporate blessing and all my human and professional understanding. What more do you want? (*Pause*) What do you want? Why are you standing as still as a pole… like the sister of your namesake, what's his name, Orestes…"

ORI: Electra?

BOSS: Right. I wanted to say light pole, but I guess electric pole would be more appropriate. Come on, drop the ladder…

ORI: I repeat, my only fault is having been born into this world.

(*He lets the rope ladder unroll into the pit.*)

BOSS: You're such a pain in the ass, Ori! I was born into this same world, too. And, just like me, so were millions of other human beings, who are also, more or less, justified in complaining about whoever created them. Listen up, because I'm talking about our loving parents – who, unfortunately for them, and for us, have come to walk in this valley of tears euphemistically called "the face the Earth," which is covered with a Carnevale mask hiding the horrible traits of a tentacled monster.

ORI: Don't leave things hanging in a fog of uncertainty; come on, give the monster a name.

BOSS: Right, you'll probably even want its address and phone number!

ORI: Life itself is already pretty sickening, so please, Boss, no need to remind me of my phone bill, too – which is also past due.

BOSS: Really? Life is sickening and your phone bill is high? I'll have to agree with you there, Ori, yet, I say: *cui prodest?* I mean, what good is complaining; who benefits from it?

ORI: It's good, it's good... especially for someone like me who has his pockets full...

BOSS: You, your pockets full? Don't make me laugh. When were your pockets ever full?

ORI: ...of problems, Boss. I meant it in a broader sense.

BOSS: Oh! You need to understand that there's nothing new about your justified, though much too random, complaints. Anyway, you know what they say; a problem shared is a problem halved. So, when it comes to your salary and your existence, my advice is to just live with it, like everyone else has to – me, first and foremo... never mind, I'll put myself second. Put your soul at ease, and stop bothering me with trifles that will pass the minute you're able to take a reassuring sip from the fountain of life.

ORI: That's easy for you to say! But the torment inside is much too strong to be quenched by a glass of water from that fountain, or a drink at some bar.

BOSS: Would you rather a smack in the head

ORI: Give me that too, and my undoing will be complete.

BOSS: Don't get down on yourself. I just hope my little talk has helped your depressed – and depressing, believe me – state of mind, so that you're now able to go down into the pit a little more, I won't say relieved, but less spiritually burdened.

ORI: Slow down. I'm starting to get tired of your fancy words.

BOSS: Fancy, you say? Well, I'm starting to tire of your misery; what am I saying, your absolute lack of will. Believe me, it's not at all fulfilling for a boss like me to give orders to a sad and cuckolded sourpuss like you.

ORI: Cuckolded and completely worn. You're absolutely right about that, Boss!

BOSS: If you say so, Ori. You're welcome. Happy Pit Day!

ORI: Happy Pit Day to you too, Boss!

(*Music*)

BLACKOUT

ACT THREE

(Inside the pit. We hear the sinister sounds of being underground. Ori drops the rope ladder from above.)

BOSS: Where do we stand, Ori?

ORI: I'm getting ready to go down.

BOSS: Then go. What are you waiting for? We're already half way through the day.

ORI: Am I insured, Boss?

BOSS: Don't bust my balls, Ori, get going. I can understand your need for security… that is, job and *social* security, but being too needy will cripple you.

ORI: No, breaking my neck will cripple me – for the rest of my life!

BOSS: Do you have your hardhat on? Yes? Then you're following all work zone regulations. Whatever happens, it can't statistically be considered the umpteenth case of death in the workplace, but just a trivial work accident widely found in the daily newspapers. But don't let what happens in other work zones scare you – here, I'm in charge.

ORI: That's exactly what scares me, Boss.

BOSS: If I say nothing will happen to you, nothing should happen to you… theoretically. Trust me.

ORI: Go tell to that to everyone I owe money to. Then, if they trust you…

BOSS: You're always going on and on!

ORI: (*Looking into the pit.*) It's not me that's going on and on, it's the ladder that's going deeper and deeper!

BOSS: It's going deeper and deeper now, because you continued to dig and dig earlier.

ORI: And I still owe lots of people. It might be better for me to hide in there forever.

BOSS: Don't be stupid. Your creditors would start asking me about you.

ORI: And would you give me up? Come on, answer. Don't leave me hanging here.

BOSS: I'm the one who hired you, so you also owe me… a debt of gratitude.

ORI: What does that mean?

BOSS: It means that even *I* am one of your creditors, my friend. Anyway, how do you plan on running away from it all?

ORI: But I don't owe *you* money.

BOSS: It was hyperbole, Ori.

ORI: I'm not even going to ask what hyperbole means, because I have bad feeling about it.

BOSS: Don't worry, hyperbole isn't dangerous. Whistle when you get to the point.

ORI: Get to the point?

BOSS: It's an expression, you idiot: the point, the bottom. Don't you know an expression when you hear one? Didn't they teach you anything in school?

ORI: Not *every single* thing.

BOSS: Right, it's a miracle you even understand the language I'm speaking.

ORI: It's not a question of the language, Boss, it's the terminology. We're not on the same wavelength, so we're having a hard time verbally communicating. We're using completely different expressive codes, even if they are *somewhat* similar. I'm speaking *Ori* and you're speaking *Boss*.

BOSS: (*Suspiciously*) This is not you talking, Ori. These are phrases you've surely heard at some union meeting. However, you should know that you're only dealing with words you don't fully understand, and that they've been fed to you on purpose to further confuse your petty ideas.

ORI: Truth is, you confused me more with that stupid "to the point."

BOSS: Stupid? I'm going to make a note that. (*He writes in a notebook*) Anyway, for your information, I meant, whistle as soon as you reach the bottom, when you reach that *point,* the summit of your descent! Understand now? A clear and simple whistle! Whistle! You reach the bottom and whistle! Is that clear?

ORI: The kind of whistle I make with my two fingers?

BOSS: Any kind of whistle, you dog!

ORI: Whistle… Dog…Got it."

BOSS: You didn't understand a fucking thing, Ori. Stop being a dickhead. You have to whistle to up *me* – not to a dog, and not even to your dick, for that matter. Understand?

ORI: Understood.

BOSS: It's about time. (*To himself*) Sometimes it takes a tow truck to move his mental abilities. How it pisses me off when he acts like this. At times he's slower than a snail!

(*Ori reaches the bottom. He looks around, frightened.*)

ORI: (*To himself.*) I knew if I listened to the Boss I'd be screwed.

BOSS: Well?

(*Ori puts both fingers in his mouth and tries to whistle, but he can't, because his hands are shaking. So, he purses his lips and lets out a faint sound. After a few moments, the Boss gets tired of waiting and shouts into the pit.*)

BOSS: Well, Ori, have you reached the fucking bottom or not?!

ORI: Yes, Boss, I'm here.

BOSS: Then, why didn't you whistle like I said.

ORI: I couldn't whistle with my two fingers, because I'm scared, and my hands are shaking too much. But, because I wanted to follow your orders precisely, I let out a little bit of a whistle… like… like the magical melody of a robin. Sorry if the expression sounds poetic.

BOSS: Hey Shakespeare, robin's chirp, they don't whistle!

ORI: What's the difference?

BOSS: There's a big difference between a two fingered whistle and a robin's chirp, Ori. You expect a faint bird call to reach me up here? And, do you know why some robins are red? Because when they emit their mating calls, they blush from embarrassment. And you! You're not even embarrassed to imitate that kind of sound? Oh, I'll give you a reason to stop screwing around with me…

ORI: But I wasn't making any kind of sexual bird sound, I was just calling up to you.

BOSS: The only thing missing today was for you to try to get my attention by using a crude sexual mating call, probably hoping I'd be lured in – hook, line and sinker – and respond by chirping back down to you. Don't get any funny ideas.

ORI: Damn all bosses and whoever gave them work.

BOSS: I heard everything, loud and clear. Now, I'm going to put you on report. You said all bosses are a "jerks."

ORI: I said "work" not "jerk," Boss. Someone must have hired you… and, yes, I'm upset with that person, and with whoever put you above me… but not with you, my direct superior."

BOSS: See how stupid you are? No one put me above you, it's you who have descended below me.

ORI: You mean, into the pit?

BOSS: Exactly

ORI: Well, if that's the case, I didn't descend willingly.

BOSS: So, it was me who made you go down there? No, Ori, I simply convinced you, by using the intellect that assists me in my position of high authority, a position of hierarchical superiority.

ORI: That's exactly what I was referring to, Boss: your rank, not your current physical position above me.

BOSS: Which doesn't excuse you from the fact that you should have used your voice to shout up to me, considering you don't know how to whistle.

ORI: But, Boss, you told me to whistle.

BOSS: And if I had told you to take flying leap into the pit, would you have done that too?

ORI: Now, I'm going to come back up there and start smacking you around!

BOSS: No, Ori, now that you're down there, there's no need for you to come back up. You don't have to prove anything to me. Avoid any acts of force, like the instinctual force of habit of coming back up without permission, which you would bitterly regret. Maybe, I'll just come down there, and lower myself to your level.

ORI: Hurry up then, it's almost lunch time.

BOSS: Is food all you think about, Ori?

ORI: When it's time to eat, yes.

BOSS: Hold the ladder, Ori. That's an direct order.

(The Boss starts to descend.)

ORI: Ok, but no one held it for me when I climbed down. The feeling of my very survival hanging in air made me doubt my own class consciousness, and a worker without class consciousness is like an acrobat suspended in a void.

BOSS: Alright then, when we climb back up, I'll go first. That way, we'll be even, and we will have followed work regulations. Your class consciousness happy now?

ORI: Nice work regulations: they were surely written by a boss just like you.

BOSS: What do you mean by that? They're not impartial enough?

ORI: What I meant was, when all is said and done, it's always us workers who get screwed.

BOSS: Stop complaining, Ori. Don't provoke the pit with your pseudo-ideological whining. Besides, class consciousness is a fairy tale no one believes in anymore – not even you. Workers like you have become part of the middle-class. They've taken all their worldly possessions and have made the pit their home – and they even like it down there."

ORI: Good for them!

BOSS: Why, aren't you happy in the pit, Ori?

ORI: I don't know. I just got here. I'll have to see how it feels first.

BOSS: Well, that's what we're here for: to inspect, measure, test out and approve the pit. Any objections?

ORI: No… not yet.

BOSS: Good.

ORI: But…

BOSS: No, no! Don't even think about it.

ORI: Forget I mentioned it, Boss.

(*The Boss reaches Ori at the bottom of the pit.*)

BOSS: So, in a nutshell, this the bottom of the pit?

ORI: In a nutshell.

BOSS: In a nutshell, what? You some kind of a parrot?

ORI: You can say "in a nutshell" and I can't?

BOSS: In a nutshell… no, you can't, absolutely not! Update me on situation, instead, you nitwit!

ORI: What?

BOSS: Didn't I send you ahead to check things out, yes or no?

ORI: If you say so.

BOSS: And what did you find, you bonehead?

ORI: That it wasn't a good idea to come down into the pit, Boss.

BOSS: We had no choice. Besides, it's not that bad down here. Don't you think?

ORI: I don't know. I can't see a thing.

BOSS: What a shame. I would've liked to have seen what the inside of a pit is made of.

ORI: Can I go back up?

BOSS: What's the hurry? Do you have something to hide?

ORI: Who? Me?

BOSS: You afraid I'm going to find out that you've excavated badly and too quickly?

ORI: The hole is here, right in front of your eyes, in its entirety.

BOSS: But, how do you know, if you just admitted that you can't see a thing?!

ORI: I mean, I can't see where it ends. What more can I say!?

BOSS: It's easy to pronounce the word, *hole*. However, there is a hole, and there is a *hole*… For instance, Ori…

(Sinister sounds emanate from the bowels of the pit.)

ORI: Yes, Boss?

BOSS: Hey, what's that noise? What does it mean?

ORI: I don't know, Boss. Maybe some type of acid reflux.

BOSS: Acid reflux? Coming fr-fr-from th-the pit?

ORI: Scared?

BOSS: No, just cautious.

ORI: Well, now you know why I didn't want to come down first.

BOSS: So, why did you make me come down second?

ORI: Because you're the Boss, and you too have to understand, or rather, be aware of what's happening in the pit.

BOSS: Ori, the pit is my responsibility when it comes to orders, shifts and the turnover of personnel. However, the interior of the pit is your work, therefore – and a "therefore" is necessary here – *therefore*, the responsibility for its construction falls squarely on you. If the pit were to suddenly collapse – let's knock as hard as possible on wood that it doesn't – but if that were to happen, who do think would be at fault? I, who have put my faith in you, or you, who have taken advantage of my unconditional trust?

ORI: Beats me!

BOSS: You cave-dwelling troglodyte! You're truly the picture-perfect image of this fucking ditch. You know what? You two are made for each other: a hot love affair right out the bowels of the pit.

ORI: Can I ask you something, Boss?

BOSS: To tell you the truth, at this crucial moment of my existence, I would rather only answers… but if you really have to ask something, then shoot.

ORI: Do you think it was a good idea, Boss?

BOSS: What, Ori? I hate answering a question with another question; it means that you either have expressed yourself poorly, or I just didn't understand well enough. What exactly are you asking?

ORI: I was asking if you think it was a good idea to come down into the pit?

BOSS: You dug it with own two hands, so if you can't tell, how do expect me to? You should know it like inside of your pockets.

ORI: I only contributed to the work. I wouldn't have been able to complete it on my own. My knowledge of the pit is limited to the very digging of it. But a pit like this isn't created on a whim: there needs to be precise planning, a reason, a motive, which I can't know in all its complexity. All I did was follow your orders to the letter. You told me to dig, and I dug – like I was possessed.

BOSS: Well, at least now you have to realize that you went a little overboard!

ORI: A little overboard?

BOSS: Yeah, you sure did! You executed the work conscientiously, I see that, for which you should receive praise. But...

ORI: But?

BOSS: You finished ahead of schedule, causing trouble for me, dammit!

ORI: I'm sorry.

BOSS: How is Pit Management going handle the problem of a ditch completed ahead of schedule?

ORI: When was the pit supposed to finished, Boss?

BOSS: I don't know! They never told me.

ORI: How could that be? You're the Boss, and they didn't officially tell you when it had to be done?

BOSS: Look, I'm not the head honcho, I'm only *your* boss – so I'm only the small head honcho above you!

ORI: I already a have a small head above me. It's the one on top of my shoulders.

BOSS: The one you have is a bonehead: it's as hard as a rock, and stubborn.

ORI: That might be true, but at least I don't send others to give my orders.

BOSS: I do, though, because that's my job. For example, I *have* to say: "You there, go tell Ori to dig." and "You, go tell him to stop…"

ORI: Well, you really never told anyone to tell me to stop. You forgot to, Boss. That's why I continued to dig, day and night, while even neglecting to fulfill my duties as a husband.

BOSS: Then it's all your fault, Ori, if the pit has turned into some kind of a monster, and your wife has turned you into a cuckold.

ORI: I guess it's nothing new, Boss.

BOSS: Of course not. You went overboard. Even excessive dedication to your work can be as counter-productive as making love 24 hours a day, 7 days week.

ORI: I thought I was doing a good job, and making a good impression on you…

BOSS: You were successful in that, Ori, and how! It was such a pleasure seeing you dig like that – as beautiful as a fireworks display – and I said to myself: "digging is in his blood." But… I just forgot you to tell to stop.

ORI: So, I worked until my hands were cut and bleeding for nothing!

BOSS: Those are just superficial grazes. You should instead look at what you've done with this pit. You've further disfigured our poor Earth's crust, which has already suffered enough at the hands of a civilization of consumerism. Why wasn't a barbarian like you just satisfied with a simple pit *sui generis*?

ORI: If you knew how tiring it was to dig, you wouldn't sum up a pit like this in just two words! *Sui generis*? Take a look how deep it is.

BOSS: I already told you, Ori. You could have taken it easy. That's right, you could have taken things slowly. You could have smoked a cigarette every now and then, you could have asked time off to take your wife to the vet… You see, that way, the excavation would have taken more time, I would have gone on being the Boss, and you would have continued to just poke around in the dirt a little at a time under my supervision. Would that have been so difficult?

ORI: Just dig poke around in the dirt a little at a time?

BOSS: What I mean is, there was no need hurry, Ori. The problem is that when someone puts a shovel in your hand, you don't think of anything else. You only think about digging. And because you continued to dig and dig, you finally hit bottom without taking into consideration the catastrophic consequences of such noble, yet counter-productive, dedication to your work.

ORI: That almost brings me to tears, Boss.

BOSS: Let this be a lesson to you, if and when you have to dig another pit.

ORI: Another pit? No, Boss, I'm done for the day – stopped, finished, on vacation.

BOSS: So, next time I tell you to dig, don't take it so seriously. That's right, take your time, and you won't skin your hands so much, and above all, you won't hit bottom too soon. What am I saying: look, we must *never* hit bottom. That way, we'll keep the construction zone open, the project will always be a work in progress, or as they say in America: WIP – that way, I'll be able to continue giving you orders, and you'll be able to obediently and indefatigably continue to dig away.

ORI: Indefatigably?

BOSS: I mean no offense. None at all!

ORI: Oh, no, who's taking offense! Especially for something as trivial as… "Indefatigably." (*Ori hasn't a clue as to the meaning of the word, "indefatigably"*)

BOSS: It's good that you acknowledge your mistakes, Ori. Now you can make amends.

ORI: The only mistake I made was to not dig a way out of this pit.

BOSS: Poor Ori, don't look for exits where there are none. There can't be any, because if there were, this would no longer be a pit, but a fun place, like an amusement park. (*Pause*) Speaking of which, have you ever taken a ride on the *Tunnel of Horrors?*"

ORI: Yes, Boss, with my wife – It was called my honeymoon.

BOSS: To be honest, I understand your existential condition of a worker on the edge of an abyss; that is, on the pit's border of imminent unemployment, and all the consequences that come with it: lack of self-esteem, a sense of loss of identity, human and social isolation, a lack of sexual activity and the subsequent fear of losing your reproductive abilities…

ORI: Meaning?

BOSS: Meaning your wife threatens to stop screwing you if you lose your job at the pit – so, in order to make the best out of a bad situation, be sure to keep your career as husband and father completely separate from the one as an incompetent worker. Don't mix your private life with your professional one; never combine the sacred with the profane… Just don't do it, Ori!

ORI: It's tough for people to separate themselves from their own human misfortunes, because they're always psychologically affected and conditioned by their surroundings – and wives who are ranting about every new utility bill.

BOSS: Well, for that matter, even the pit's walls are closing in on you, but you don't seem to take that too seriously.

ORI: It does have a bad effect on me, Boss. I would really like to fill it back in. I'd work day and night for free, if you gave me, I won't say the order, but a little permission to do so. Its very existence offends my intelligence.

BOSS: Excuse me, Ori, but what are you talking about?

ORI: About my… never mind, forget it, Boss! You wouldn't understand.

BOSS: You think I wouldn't understand, you scoundrel? Do you think I don't see what's in this pit; that there's nothing at all in here? Do you think the very concept of the pit fulfills my human ambitions and professional aspirations? Of course you do, why wouldn't you! Do you think I'm satisfied? When I was young, I broke my ass to study and graduate from college with honors; raise a family; feed and give my kids a weekly allowance; educate them by enrolling them in school and sports; only to end up digging a damn underground hole full of nothing? What a great goal! Oh no, my friend, that's not the case at all! The abyss below one's feet opens very slowly. At first you see nothing but a starry sky, maybe some overhanging clouds every now and then, but nothing serious, you understand. Sooner or later, those clouds clear, and once you see the twinkling stars reappear, you reach for them again, though with greater strength, and you are thrust in a world of ideals, hopes, dreams and illusions. Yes, stupid and empty illusions, because all of a sudden you wake from your drunkenness. And where do find yourself? Well, an example is right in front of you: in a pit, from which you can now only barely glimpse a small part of that sky you used to dream of in your youth. Take me, for example: I studied aerospace engineering, I wanted to send rockets to the most faraway planets. Instead, look how low I've sunk... into your filthy pit.

ORI: Is that a confession, Boss?

BOSS: I hope you weren't recording this. Keep it quiet, Ori. I wasn't taking an official position, just getting some personal things off my chest that must absolutely stay *inter nos* – between us.

ORI: But I think the same way you do.

BOSS: Then, do you understand why I can't give you neither the order nor the permission to fill in the hole? The pit is now a set and incontrovertible fact. I told you to dig it. You dug it. Now it exists. What's done is done, and a boss can't undo it.

ORI: And you be would that Boss?

BOSS: And, you, that worker.

ORI: The one who always gets screwed!

BOSS: You're complaining? Not happy? Unfortunately for you – and a little for me too – there's no other alternative. Reality doesn't change according to our wishes and personal states of mind. You would need more, Ori, a lot more to fill in this disgusting pit that was created by your shovel. We would need…

ORI: A counter-order, Boss. That would do it.

BOSS: What are you talking about?

ORI: Just as you gave me the order to dig, now you could simply give me the order to fill it in. The order to fill instead of to dig, that's all.

BOSS: And who's going to authorize me to give you that order, imbecile? An order isn't created on its own. It has to follow the correct procedure. It has to be passed around, discussed, then it has to reach the right ears.

ORI: You just have to say, "fill it in," and get it over with.

BOSS: I can't. I'm afraid to. Even if I were able, and not scared, I wouldn't do it. Why? Because something more monstrous could emerge in its place.

ORI: Worse than the pit?

BOSS: Who can say for sure, either way? Things can always be worse, Ori. Anyway, once we fill it in, then what? We just head home and forget about our salaries?

ORI: What do you mean? We could then just freelance and ask a flat rate to dig up a smaller hole… if you want.

BOSS: Why would you fill it in if you just dug it up? And why would you dig it up again if you just filled it in? I don't understand the reason for such efforts. We'd be right back where we started.

ORI: No. Listen to me! We'll make a bunch of little holes, Boss. Then if anyone asks: "Are you digging?" you'll be able to answer in good conscience: "Yes, we're digging! And how we're digging!"

BOSS: And what if someone wants details and asks: "What are you digging?" How would I answer, huh? That the first pit was excavated poorly, so now we are correcting the problem by digging another? No, Ori, let's think carefully before taking some irreversible action that could jeopardize a reputation built up over many years of an honest career. Let's leave the pit as it is… at least for now. If the moment comes when we have to act, *then* we'll decide what to do. Maybe we'll dig an inground pool, who knows? (*Pause*) Speaking of pools, I need to take a piss. Certain images have a strange effect on me.

(*The Boss steps aside and turns with his back to the audience.*)

ORI: If we don't make a definitive decision right now – that of filling in the pit – we might never be able to escape it. We'll fall deeper into its maze, deeper into the void, which, for the moment, is hidden by a bottom that only seems solid, but that could suddenly become swampy and muddy… in short, not firm enough to support the weight of our conscience.

(*The Boss has finished and is buttoning up his pants. Ori starts dusting off his dirty boots.*)

BOSS: Ah! Conscience! You have a dirty conscience? That's why the pit scares you so much! I agree that this pit is worse than all the pits that came before it, because of its stupidity and lack of values. It's become terrifying, and it's truly difficult to understand its deeper meaning, but the fact that it's turned out this way is destiny. Because, unfortunately for you, Ori, the pit is in your blood, or rather, in your head. That's why you hate it so much: because it been part of you since you were born. There's a sinkhole in your heart, Ori, acknowledge it.

ORI: Fact is, I do remember the pit ever since I was born. That would explain my hate and disgust. It forced me to be born, it gave me this rotten life, it flung me into a world where I only found another pit, greater, more repugnant and more hostile than the one I came out of against my will.

BOSS: Really? This pit has that much of an effect on your imagination? Does it unleash your most profound anguish? Does it awaken in you a most insidious dream state that leads to absolute and cerebral onanism?

ORI: Excuse me?

BOSS: Let me explain. In your childhood subconscious, the pit represents the vaginal cavity through which you were born, and to which you now have an obvious desire to return. Be sincere, Ori, tell me from the heart, am I right? Be honest. No one can hear us down here. Just speak softly, as if you were at confession.

ORI: I'm just saying that the pit could have turned out better than it did. That's why it should be filled in and dug up again – from start, Boss!

BOSS: Dug up again! Why would you want to dig it again?

ORI: Because it's a lacking a foundation.

BOSS: What do you know about foundations?

ORI: Intuition, Boss – but I'm always right on the money.

BOSS: Are you saying the pit is unsound?

ORI: Yes.

BOSS: But you dug it.

ORI: I dug it, but I didn't lay a foundation.

BOSS: What are your work responsibilities? Answer, you moron.

ORI: To dig.

BOSS: And did you dig?

ORI: And how!

BOSS: Now we'll find out if and how you dug, considering you're complaining about the hole that you yourself made. Let's measure its size… after all, we came down here to inspect, check, measure and report.

ORI: Report to who?

BOSS: Whoever's in charge up there.

ORI: How do you expect to report to someone above, if no one pulls you up and out of here first?

BOSS: Congratulations, Ori, that's a good question.

ORI: And?

BOSS: (*Smiling condescendingly*) Dammit! Don't create problems that don't directly or personally involve you… and never mind laying a foundation in a bottomless pit, which, as the words imply, can never have one! It's threatening, crumbling, dangerous, and always on the brink of swallowing up everything and everyone. Otherwise, you wouldn't call it a bottomless pit, but rather a hotel room, a restaurant, a club, or, better yet, a pizzeria – in that case, it would be a place of enjoyment, and not of death and sufferance, which it truly seems to be. To make sense of the pit is like looking for reason in your farts, Ori, which are nothing but thin air – just like all your rebellious worker complaints. You're never satisfied: "the shovel is too short," "The wheel barrel is too heavy," "That brick is too crooked," "The wood is too wet," and "The pit is too always deep." (*Pause*) Stay still, Ori, don't move…

ORI: What… do you see a snake? Oh no, I'm going to end up like poor Orestes, who was bitten by…

BOSS: Stop saying Orestes, Ori! There's no snake. I have to measure the pit, and I need you to be a point of reference for me.

ORI: I have to be a point of reference for you? (*Sincerely*) What an honor.

BOSS: It might strange, but that's the way it is. There's always a first for everything. But don't get delusions of grandeur, this will be the first and last time you'll be a point of reference for me.

ORI: What do I have to do?

BOSS: You don't even know how to act as a point of reference – like a marking stick, you imbecile? You just have to stand still, upright, like you're at attention! Haven't you ever played Capture the Flag when you were a kid? (*Ori nods.*) Good, you have to act like the flag.

ORI: Me?

BOSS: Yeah, you. (*Ori stands upright and erect. The Boss takes three steps.*) One, two, three… (*He stops, exhausted.*)

ORI: Happy?

BOSS: My God, it's really immense, huge, apocalyptic. I'm drenched in sweat. How many steps did I count? A thousand? Two thousand? And I didn't even get halfway across. What the hell is it even good for?

ORI: Now you're asking me? It's been forever that I've have been asking you to explain the nature and meaning of the pit.

BOSS: You have more direct experience with it than I do, that's why I'm asking you for answers. Even if they're only opinions or personal views, just something to take into account – loosely, of course, because your ignorant impressions aren't too useful in general.

ORI: But I…

BOSS: I only gave you the order to dig, but it was you who physically did it. I understand your justifiable objection. I was rough on you just now for having perceived the urgency of needing to give meaning and a foundation to the pit. All of a sudden, though, I, myself, can't find a logical explanation, or understand even the smallest detail of the project as a whole. I'm not losing it, Ori, trust me. It's just that I didn't want you to so openly, brazenly or visibly look for the damn meaning in things, so that you – and I, indirectly – wouldn't make a bad impression. You might ask how we could make a bad impression? I'll tell you how. The higher ups might ask: "Why would you have dug this much, and given so many orders to dig, without knowing the reason or purpose for the pit, or even the nature of it? Have you become such fools as to dig under these circumstances?" You understand, Ori?

ORI: I know the reason for my efforts: it's called a salary. But when it comes to you, do you know why you gave me order to dig? Was it only for the salary, or was it something else?

BOSS: How am I supposed to know? Do you think I know the reason and meaning of the orders I have to give? No one tells me anything, Ori. The order is to dig, and that's precisely why I tell you to dig. An order that is unclear to you is the same for me. It's just that in executing the order to dig, you're can understand its meaning, the end point, the goal – the reason you were given the order in the first place. It's easy for you! You just live with it. You dig a black hole, and as you continue burrowing down, you understand all whys and wherefores. If nothing else, the pit, the hole, the ditch, or whatever you want to call it, is an unalienated product of your work, and it provides you just enough to get by. It's different for me, because the pit isn't mine: I don't own the land above it, I don't own the empty space created by it, and, unlike you, I can't say I've spiritually developed because of it. It means nothing; it's obscure and foreign to me. It's just a stupid, empty pit without meaning, and if I weren't your boss, I'd just be someone else's boss – maybe someone who's working on... I don't know... building a rocket bound for Pluto.

ORI: A choice planet, Boss.

BOSS: Funny, but that's the first place that came to mind. Who knows why? Maybe it's the association with the letter P: Pit – Pluto, Pluto – Pit!

ORI: Well, the meaning of the pit is that it has no meaning at all.

(There's a pause of puzzling reflection.)

BOSS: Ori, you amaze me.

ORI: Why thank you, Boss.

BOSS: Don't thank me. You amaze me, but not in the way you think.

ORI: Meaning?

BOSS: Meaning it's no compliment. You piss me off. And you know why? Because you spout out stupid comments in such a serious way that they seem like profound concepts, though coming from someone who only knows how to tell vulgar jokes. For instance, explain this umpteenth smart-ass opinion, this bullshit about the pit not having any meaning at all. You screwing around with me again?

ORI: Does the pit have a meaning, in your opinion?

BOSS: No, for God's sake, it does not!

ORI: So, what sense was there in digging it?

BOSS: None.

ORI: Then, you agree that the meaning of the pit is that it has no meaning at all.

BOSS: Well, why did you dig it?

ORI: Why did you tell me to dig it?

BOSS: Why didn't you refuse to dig it? Because, you benefited: by digging it, you got paid, right?

ORI: Why didn't you refuse to tell me to dig it? Because you benefited: by giving the order, it made you feel like some god on a pedestal, right?

BOSS: Listen, I've come to the conclusion that you should be strangled right here on the work site, before you're able to do anymore damage. That's right! I'm officially in favor of your physical elimination from the pit. (*The Boss starts to strangle Ori.*) Plus, it's a matter of the safety and mental health of the other workers who, I agree, are also trying to find a definitive meaning in the pit. But even if they don't find one, they don't taint it with worker defeatism and aren't in constant disagreement with both the employers and the union. Instead, they protest in silence, like a hunger strike, which doesn't hurt anyone, not even those involved. On the contrary!

ORI: Boss, you're choking the life out of me.

BOSS: Yes, Ori, I am chocking you to death. May your soul rest in peace.

ORI: You're doing this now that a meaning is starting to take shape?

BOSS: A meaning? For you or for me?

ORI: For both of us, I think.

(*We hear the sound of a gong. The Boss stops strangling Ori.*)

BOSS: And in your opinion, that would be a sign?

ORI: Maybe it's a bad sign.

BOSS: So, I shouldn't continue strangling you?

ORI: It's definitely proof.

BOSS: Proof? Of what?

ORI: Proof that there is a meaning. I agree, it might obscure and unclear, but it's there.

BOSS: I've had it up to here with those two or three philosophical views you have, which you hope to use to win some TV quiz show.

ORI: Calm down, Boss. Philosophy, even that of a simple worker like me, has a precise function.

BOSS: What's that, Ori? Tell me, before I carry out your death sentence.

ORI: Its function is to give meaning to something like the pit that doesn't seem to have any meaning at all.

BOSS: It's strangling time! (*He starts strangling the worker again.*)

ORI: Without philosophy, we wouldn't be able to interpret the very essence of phenomena, Boss. That's the way it is.

BOSS: Essence? What are you talking about?

ORI: The essence of meaning.

BOSS: You know what I have to say? I'm not going strangle you. (*He stops and removes his hands from the worker's neck.*) That's right, you understood perfectly; I'm going to desist from the objective of wringing your neck like a chicken. You are quite the living proof of the most extraordinary example of human stupidity. Why would I strangle you? It's more fitting to show you off as one of the most abominable and unnerving products of the pit, wouldn't you think?

ORI: The pit is a product of my work, and not vice versa. Although…

BOSS: Dear God, there's an even an "although!"

ORI: Although, theoretically, the meaning, or rather, the concept of the pit should predate both of us.

BOSS: Predate me? How dare you?!

ORI: It's in the very own logic of things. If the concept of the pit had never existed, we wouldn't have even thought of digging it. It might sound strange, but that's the way it is.

BOSS: Ori, I've thought things over again; I might just strangle you after all. (*His hand reaches for the worker's throat.*)

ORI: Calm down, Boss. (*The Boss stops.*) Even you have to consider it from a philosophical point of view, because it helps to understand how things really are – or how they are not. Or else, how they were, but are no longer. Do you want a good example?

BOSS: Go ahead, give me a good example.

ORI: (*Pause*)… The ladder.

BOSS: What ladder? What does a ladder have to do with your example?

ORI: It has nothing to do with my example. I'm talking about the rope ladder we used to climb down.

BOSS: What about it?

ORI: It's gone… They must have pulled it up without telling us, maybe as a joke, or because they didn't see us down here.

BOSS: Why didn't you pay more attention!? Damn you and all your literary salon talk, to which I stupidly contributed!

ORI: I'm only trying to help, Boss.

BOSS: I should have killed you immediately. In a moment of spiritual crisis, you even squeezed a mini-confession out of me about my deepest fears. I didn't realize that the greatest danger isn't the pit itself. No, Ori… the real danger is you, who digs these ditches. Someone gave you an inch and you took a mile…

ORI: And someone else took the ladder.

BOSS: If I hadn't stayed here listening to your theories, maybe the ladder wouldn't have disappeared, and we'd be able climb back out. Now, though, everything has gotten so damn complicated. You've contributed to the creation of a great story ending: the disappearance of the ladder! Your philosophy has carried us out of this world, out of reality. We've been swallowed up by the pit, Ori, and now we're cut off from everything. We no longer have a reason to exist. Trust me!

ORI: Maybe you don't, but I do.

BOSS: You? What reason do you have?

ORI: To survive, Boss.

BOSS: Under these conditions?

ORI: Always and forever: survival is my motto, making ends meet is my job. And you know what I do? I survive and make ends meet.

BOSS: To tell you the truth, that life philosophy seems simple and effective. I congratulate you, Ori. I'll bet it was me who hired you. Who else, other than myself, could have perceived the crude, yet pragmatic brilliance, of a jackass like you.

ORI: Actually, you wanted to fire me. Worse, you wanted to physically get rid of me.

BOSS: How did we ever get to this point… and why?

ORI: Because I accidentally hit the bottom of the pit. Don't you remember?

BOSS: That's in the past, water under the bridge. I've now determined that you're not a complete imbecile. A small dose of crystal-clear sense glimmers in you – even if it's amidst a sea of intellectual mud, let's be honest!

ORI: Thank you, Boss! Thank you… coming from you, that's great professional recognition.

Every now and then, even a simple worker like me needs a pat on the back – and a raise.

BOSS: I'll give you all the pats you want. When it comes to the raise, we'll talk about that when you're successful in getting me out of this pit you've created.

(*We hear the sound of a gong.*)

ORI: Should we call for help?

BOSS: Someone sounds a gong, and you want to immediately call for help?

ORI: I, too, would like to get out of this pit as soon as possible, out of this horrible existential situation, before they place an immovable gravestone above us.

BOSS: I don't think it's necessary to speak of graves. Don't you agree, Ori?

ORI: Fully, Boss.
BOSS: Then, let's set things straight, considering we might be stuck down here for a while.

ORI: Ok, let's do that.

BOSS: Rule number one – the one that states we can't mention graves – is unanimously approved.

ORI: A unanimous vote, wonderful! — though not that's not too difficult considering there are only two of us!

BOSS: Look, Ori, me agreeing with you and, above all, you agreeing with someone that's not yourself, is an historical event, momentous. Biblical…

ORI: Let's move on to rule number two, if you don't mind. I can't wait to make some rules of my own.

BOSS: What do you have to do with the rules?

ORI: What's wrong with each of us making a rule. That's the basis for democracy.

BOSS: And who told you this is a democracy?

ORI: Isn't it?

BOSS: It could be, but that has yet to be decided.

ORI: And who decides?

BOSS: Me.

ORI: And who decides that you decide.

BOSS: Me.

ORI: And me?

(*The gong sounds again, though louder than before.*)

ORI: Maybe someone up there is trying to tell us it's time for lunch.

BOSS: Good. If *they're* saying it, then I've no problem in repeating it: LUNCH! Grab you your lunchbox, Ori.

ORI: I left it up in the work zone, Boss.

BOSS: What? You make me call lunch, and you don't have anything to eat?

ORI: It was just assumed it was lunch, Boss, but I was certain.

BOSS: Great! So, we'll fill our stomachs with your stupid assumptions!

(*A prosciutto and sausages rain from above.*)

ORI: At least the cafeteria cuts the mustard.

BOSS: The philosopher, Benedetto Croce, explains unknowable reality by comparing it to unreachable hanging salamis that can be smelled, but not seen.

ORI: We're talking about simple cold cuts here, Boss, and not true ideals.

BOSS: So, in your opinion, a sausage can't consist of an ideal? If you have to be a rotten materialist, at least look to history, Ori.

ORI: Why history, Boss?

BOSS: Because when a sausage falls, you shouldn't just see a falling sausage! It is possible you don't realize that a falling sausage, with its background and premises, is much more complex than it seems.

ORI: Sausages are raining down at lunchtime, like falling abstract ideals, and you're complaining?

BOSS: And if they are neither ideals nor true sausages?

ORI: Then what could they be?

BOSS: They could be our values that are falling, Ori.

ORI: They're sausages, trust me.

BOSS: We're better off then.

ORI: I might only be a shadow closed up in a platonic cavern, from which they made a ladder disappear that would have served to climb back up to reality, but I have such a pit in my stomach that I have no choice but to consider a sausage a sausage.

BOSS: This time, you're completely right, Ori.

ORI: Thank you, Boss. Bon Appétit.

BOSS: First, though, let's pay humble and pious homage to reality. Pray with me, Ori.

ORI: Damn, such a fuss for a piece of prosciutto!

BOSS: Quiet. Let's pray.

ORI: Let's pray then!

BOSS: *(The Boss glimpses at him, then quickly prays without articulating the words clearly.)* Blah, blah, blah… done.

ORI: Amen. Finally, let's eat.

(Ori and the Boss eat.)

BOSS: I want to tell you a you a secret, Ori; be sure to keep it to yourself, though. I wouldn't want my small corporate position smeared by a compromising statement made in my current inspirational full stomach state of mind: I hate the reality that surrounds me. To me, the world seems like a torn, pompous and badly painted backdrop for some nonsensical theater. I'd like to break through that backdrop, Ori, come out the other side, and see what exists behind the world's stage. (*Pause*) I'm sorry, but did I say something already too evident for you not to applaud?

ORI: Boss, clean up please.

BOSS: You think that's nice?

ORI: Well, I set up for lunch.

BOSS: Maybe I should even wash the dishes.

ORI: Ok, I'll dry them when you're done.

BOSS: There's not even a dishwasher in this damn pit?

(*All of a sudden, a dishwasher falls from above.*)

ORI: See? It's happened again. Someone has thrown an old dishwasher into the pit, and who knows if it even works.

BOSS: And you're complaining?

ORI: I just find it a little depressing, that's all.

BOSS: That I don't have to wash the dishes? You envious bastard. When good fortune comes my way, it burns your ass. Venom bursts from your every pore, Ori. Restrain yourself.

ORI: It's not good fortune that's coming your way, and it's not venom that's bursting from my pores – I'm afraid someone has taken our pit for a garbage dump… and they're even pissing down from above.

BOSS: What pigs!

ORI: I worked so hard under the illusion that I was creating something truly useful, a pit full of symbolic and metaphysical meaning, and then all of a sudden, I'm facing the undeniable fact that I only created a giant trash bin. It's not made of metaphors and ideals, just trash, garbage, leftovers, remnants, worms and sewer rats… just like us!

BOSS: Like you. Don't you dare mix the authority I represent in with your ideological and moralistic debris.

ORI: Don't you ever get sick of being the boss?

BOSS: Why would I, for God's sake? Being the boss is wonderful and rewarding.

ORI: Even digging can be rewarding.

BOSS: Don't worry, Ori, I have no intention of taking your job.

(*All of a sudden, we again hear the sound of the gong.*)

ORI: There it is again; that gong we can't fully understand.

BOSS: It was a call to order, Ori.

ORI: What order?

BOSS: Established order; that which tells you how, when and why the lunch break has come to an end.

ORI: The lunch break is over? Really?

BOSS: Yes, unfortunately.

ORI: That's a shame.

BOSS: Take comfort in this simple, yet appropriate, thought: That which begins must also come to an end.

ORI: That's not much of a comfort.

BOSS: I don't know any other way to put it.

ORI: Neither do I.

BOSS: Then, let's get to work.

ORI: What work?

BOSS: What do you mean, "What work?"

ORI: I understood what you said, Boss, but what do I have to do?

BOSS: You don't know what you have to do?

ORI: Me? No. Do you know what you need me to do?

BOSS: Damn you, Ori! (*He hits Ori on the arm.*)

ORI: Why are you hitting me? What did I do?

BOSS: Nothing! That's the problem.

ORI: You love giving orders and being in charge, but God forbid you should know what orders to give when it comes time to exercise your authority, which you claim was given to you from higher up. I'd like to know from how high this authority comes!

BOSS: So, if I don't give orders, you refuse to obey. Is that the way it is, you dirty traitor?

ORI: I'm not refusing to obey… it's just that I can't obey something if I don't know what that something is.

BOSS: Fact is, you're unable to understand on your own what needs to be done.

ORI: I'm not paid to understand on my own.

BOSS: Then what are paid for?

ORI: To dig.

BOSS: And are you digging?

ORI: Not at the moment, no.

BOSS: You see, you're a slacker!

(*All of sudden, we hear the sound of the gong yet again.*)

ORI: Is it upset with us again, Boss?

BOSS: Yes, Ori, it wants you to start doing some *generic* work, and it wants me to show you how.

ORI: *Generic* work?

BOSS: Come on, make something up. Pretend to work. Otherwise, you're going to get me, your boss, in trouble too. I can already hear them up there: "You should have kept an eye on him!" or

"You should have realized what a mess he was making!"

ORI: Who?

BOSS: The supervisors.

ORI: Aren't you the supervisor.

BOSS: When it comes to you, yes, I am. But when it comes to me, there are other supervisors.

ORI: So, you're not as much of a supervisor as you say you are.

BOSS: You're pitiful, Ori. We've fallen into this damn pit, my friend, because of your superficiality and a chronic lack of deep spirituality and human solidarity. You don't even have the least bit of respect for the authority represented by this uniform. You have clumsily dragged me into the bowels of the Earth, which is just a symbol of the nothingness inside you. You even got screwed out of the ladder that would have allowed us to climb back out to the reality above. I'm sick and tired of everything: tired of you, tired of your wife, tired of Orestes and his sister, tired of this pit, this cove, tired of…

(*A stove falls from above.*)

ORI: Sorry, Boss, did you want gas or electric?

BOSS: I said cove, not stove. I don't think I ever said stove. I would have remembered, dammit!

ORI: And yet, they sent us a stove.

BOSS: (*Hysterically*) We don't need it, I didn't order one, let them come and take it back!

ORI: Well, if they've thrown it into the pit, it means they don't know what else to do with it, otherwise, they would have surely kept it. A stove can always be of use…

BOSS: I hate to tell you, Ori, but you made a fucking mess of things by digging this pit. It looks like a garbage dump both outside and inside. It's your fault if they're throwing in all the rubbish they no longer need, you included. As for me, I just can't wait to get out of here, dammit. This is a cursed bottomless pit without an exit.

ORI: Should we call for help now?

BOSS: On no, I'm not calling for help. Me call for help? You have an inferiority complex, Ori. However, if I have to get out of a mess, a hole, a disgusting pit, which I, more or less, unintentionally got myself into, I'll do it completely on my own, using my professional and entrepreneurial abilities. I've hit bottom, but I can't throw my skills into question, I can't lower myself and accept aid, assistance, or believe in hypothetical miracles to get up and out of here. I'll use my own limbs to climb out. Mark my words!

ORI: How?

BOSS: Grab the shovel and start digging. (*He's hit with more falling garbage.*) Hurry up, before they bury us in filth, dammit!

ORI: But didn't you just say you would use your own limbs to climb out?

BOSS: Exactly.

ORI: Then, why do I have to dig?

BOSS: You want to get out, too, don't you? Yes or no?

ORI: But by digging, I'm going in the opposite direction. If I dig, I'll be going down, instead of going up.

BOSS: Follow orders. Don't you dare make a fuss. Be careful, or I'll make a note of it.

ORI: And what do you want me to reach?

BOSS: The other side, stupid.

ORI: Of what?

BOSS: Of the pit. We'll end up somewhere, sooner or later.

ORI: Sooner or later, we'll end up in Hell.

BOSS: You have no sense of geography, Ori. To get to Hell, first you have to die. This has been happening from the beginning of time. Trust me.

ORI: I'm better off not trusting you, Boss.

BOSS: Listen. If you had studied engineering, like I did, you would know the Principle of Communicating Vessels. Since you lack theory, though, I'll explain it with a practical example. You know when someone eats bean from a can?

ORI: Yes, Boss.

BOSS: The beans go in one end, and the other end emits a gaseous exhaust.

ORI: I'm not a gaseous exhaust, nor a bean.

BOSS: But you move your bowels like most, almost all, of mankind. Right?

ORI: I can't deny that.

BOSS: So, you have to admit that everything that goes in has to eventually come out somewhere, right? So, if we're not able to exit, rise from ashes the way we came in, through the mouth of the pit, then we'll certainly escape through its rear end, like the canned beans I just talked about. You understand the concept?

ORI: No, Boss. The example doesn't convince me.

BOSS: No one wants to convince you. Shut up and dig. That's an order.

ORI: If you're giving me the unconditional order to dig, I'll dig, but only because I have to. The plan doesn't add up, but you are forcing me to do it.

BOSS: Good man, Ori, that's the way I like you: an obedient worker who knows his place.

ORI: I'm not one who knows his place, but one that's always getting screwed, Boss.

BOSS: Precisely, Ori. And you'll see, you'll even start to like it. I'm sure of it. Have some faith. It's question of time. Sooner or later, everyone likes it: no one will waffle, whether good looking or awful.

ORI: I hope not, Boss.

BOSS: Live and learn, Ori.

(Ori starts digging again. The Boss suspiciously checks his work.)

ORI: Boss?

BOSS: Yes, Ori? What's up? What's going on? You didn't by chance exit the other side of the pit, did you?

ORI: Can I say something?

BOSS: Provided you say something serious and intelligent.

ORI: I have to fart.

BOSS: That's something serious and intelligent? Shame on you!

ORI: But I can't hold it.

BOSS: Then it's all crap and not a simple fart. I'm sorry, but you're going to have to hold it in, at least until we've gotten out of here. Thing is, the pit is poorly ventilated, because it only consists of a single hole. That's why I'm having you dig another, so that even you can express yourself spiritually, fully and freely. Hurry up, though. For your own sake. Work, work, work!

ORI: I'm working, for heaven's sake!

BOSS: Good. Anyway, you have no choice!

ORI: Be honest, Boss, whose side are you on, mine or the pit's?

BOSS: Ori, you amaze me. What do you mean whose side am I on? I'm bipartisan, Ori. I'm on both sides. I think you're somewhat right, and I think the pit's somewhat right. You have to understand that the truth doesn't fall solely on one side. You complain that the pit is too deep, and the pit complains that you have just dug too much. You have to find a middle-ground – the reasoning on both sides. I probably seem like a vile opportunist to you, Ori, but I am just being wise: I speak poorly of you to the pit, and speak poorly of the pit when I speak well of you. It's as simple as that. I balance myself Ori, on the edge of the abyss – constantly in play!

ORI: I congratulate you on such acrobatic skills!

BOSS: You're being ironic, but you see, there's only one outcome: I continue to be in charge, and you, on the other hand, continue to dig, pauper that you are.

ORI: Can I at least ponder things while I dig?

BOSS: Can I prohibit you from doing so? No? Then, let your thoughts rip.

(*Ori continues to dig. We then hear a farting sound.*)

BOSS: Ori, how dare you? I told you there's no farting in the pit!

ORI: You said, "Let your thoughts rip." That's what I was thinking about, so I let it rip… into thin air.

BOSS: Let different thoughts rip, then. Can you do that?

ORI: I'll try.

(*Ori digs.*)

BOSS: I still smell the strong aroma of gas.

ORI: The strong *aroma*, Boss?

BOSS: It's a euphemism. I should have said stench, but I didn't want to openly disgrace you, Ori. Control yourself.

ORI: Does euphemism mean I did it?

BOSS: Forget it. (*The Boss lies back and dozes off for a minute, while Ori continues to dig. He then awakens.*) Well, have you reached the other side of the pit? Once you've created another hole, we'll have some ventilation. Boy, we really need fresh air in here!

ORI: I haven't finished yet, Boss. The bottom of the pit is really hard. I'm only able to graze it with the shovel.

BOSS: Why didn't you bring the pneumatic hammer?

ORI: I thought that would have too much, Boss.

BOSS: Worse for you. You would have finished a lot quicker. Don't leave for tomorrow what you can do today, Ori.

ORI: I, personally, don't have any time to lose. You, on the other hand, did you have a good nap, at least?

BOSS: I don't know. I had a strange sensation. While I was sleeping, I felt – you'll never believe it, even I hesitate to admit such nonsense – but I felt afraid. You heard me right, Ori. There was a moment there when I felt afraid of dying. I'm ashamed to even tell you…

ORI: Don't to be ashamed. Maybe you need to have a fear of dying to feel truly alive. Maybe that's the meaning or purpose of the pit: Fear.

BOSS: You might be right. The darkness of the pit, and the strange rumblings and creaking sounds are like a skeleton crumbling to pieces.

Do you think you've stumbled onto some catacomb, Ori?

ORI: No, boss. It's not the creaking of a human skeleton.

BOSS: What can it be then, for heaven's sake?

ORI: It's the skeleton of the pit, Boss.

BOSS: The skeleton of the pit? Ori, you bungler, what did you end up excavating while I took the liberty of taking a short, but well-deserved nap?

ORI: Nothing, Boss.

BOSS: What do you mean, nothing? *(The rumblings get louder.)* We're no longer hearing just rumblings, but loud booms.

ORI: Boss, you have to relay the unfortunate news that the pit is falling to pieces.

BOSS: To Pieces? The Pit? Fuck, this is a nightmare – and you, Ori, are the monster in it.

ORI: Goodbye, Boss. The pit is collapsing.

BOSS: Farewell, Ori. And once we've reached the afterlife, I don't ever want to see you again. Understand?

THE PIT

(Ori strikes the pit one last time with the shovel, causing its total collapse. We hear an explosive boom.)

BLACKOUT

FINALE

(The pit is gone. Once the dust settles, we see Ori and the Boss, semi-buried under the rubble, regain consciousness. They are complaining.)

BOSS: Damn you, Ori! Look what you done! You're going to pay for this, you bastard!

ORI: First you tell me to dig, then you change your mind, yell at me and ask why I dug! First you call me a slacker who doesn't show up for work, then you immediately accuse me of working too hard just for show, in order to get a raise! You're playing the blame game, without letting me finish my job, nor allowing me to even do it at all! Nice situation we have here!

BOSS: To do your job badly is like not doing your job at all. Truth is, you're just a damn blockhead. You dug a pit within the pit, as was requested, fine, but did you reinforce it?

ORI: I didn't think of reinforcing it, because it seemed abstract and surreal enough to hold itself up on its own.

BOSS: Instead, it didn't hold up, you stubborn mule, because even metaphors require solid foundations. And who has to lay these foundations: he who digs, or he who gives you the order to dig? Your pit was worthless. It collapsed like a sand castle on the shores of a beach. There's nothing left for you to do but start over again and dig another one.

ORI: Isn't one enough?

BOSS: It would have been 100% enough, if you hadn't tempted fate by elevating it to a symbol of your existential condition. You brought to light its oneiric traits, which it didn't even know it had. But, now, that the dream has transformed itself into a nightmare, and the nightmare into a catastrophe of planetary dimensions. The pit has to be dug up again for it to assume the right size for public use. Dig, Ori, dig, and don't stop digging.

ORI: And while I'm digging, what are you going to do, Boss?

BOSS: I'll consider what we'll need to do post-pit, Ori… if something even exists after the pit. And don't forget to do a job worthy of merit.

ORI: I'll do my best, Boss. I've starting digging.

BOSS: Good man, Ori. That's the way I like you: digging and not talking.

ORI: Thanks for saying that, Boss.

BOSS: No problem. You're welcome. Now, get to work.

(Ori starts to glumly dig again. Music. Fadeout.)

CURTAIN

Enrico
Bernard
(Rome, 11 November 1955)

by Rocco Capozzi
University of Toronto

Among the new contemporary voices of Italian theater Enrico Bernard stands out as one of the most successful playwrights to impress audiences and critics alike with practically every new play that he staged, mostly in Roman theatres, throughout the Eighties, Nineties and into the New Millennium. His move from cabaret entertainer to the stage came easily for him. He possessed a background in music, had studied philosophy, German literature and European theater, and was raised in an ambience of artists and intellectuals. Enrico Bernard's knowledge of German exposed him to the works of Ludwig Tieck and Friedrich von Schiller who together with his other favorite authors and playwrights such as Carlo Goldoni, Luigi Pirandello, Samuel Becket, Eugene Ionesco, and Antonin Artaud; have played a major influence in his own playwriting. He has written over twenty theatrical texts of which thirteen have been staged in Italy and one, *Un mostro di nome Lila* (A Monster Named Lila, 1995) was performed in Italy, Austria, France, and Switzerland. After the overwhelming success of *Un mostro di nome Lila* both on stage and on the screen, his plays are beginning to be translated outside of Italy in French, German and English.

Playwright, film-maker, editor, translator, and journalist, Enrico was born in Rome on 11 November, 1955. He is the youngest of three sons of the author Carlo Bernari (pseudonym of Carlo Bernard, 1908-1992). Enrico grew up in rich and lively cultural surroundings that strongly influenced his early education and his overall artistic drive in the fields of journalism, theater, literature, and cinema. Carlo Bernari's home-studio in Rome was a favorite meeting place for illustrious authors, journalists and artists with whom young Enrico came in frequent contact especially throughout the sixties and seventies. The author's voracious curiosity about the world of art and literature has its origins in his high school years when he would be invited quite often by his father's remain to stay in the study-room and be part of the discussions. Among the many acquaintances that influenced the young man in his formative years and during his college days, in addition to narrators like Vasco Pratolini, Domenico Rea, Michele Prisco, or Giuseppe Cassieri; were the playwright Eduardo De Filippo, poets Elio Filippo Accrocca and Alfonso Gatto; film directors such as Cesare Zavattini, Nanni Loy and Pietro Germi; painters including Paolo Ricci, Emilio Greco, Ettore de Conciliis, and Alberto Sughi; and several literary critics, in particular Giuliano Manacorda and Giacinto Spagnoletti.

Bernard's interdisciplinary education received a strong foundation between 1971 and 1976, at the well known Roman secondary school, the Liceo Scientifico Castelnovo whose school president at the time was the distinguished humanist and literary critic Carlo Salinari.

During the student revolution years of 1968-1969 Salinari had begun to transform the school into a university-like learning center as he would invite important professors and high profile specialists from different disciplines as guest teachers. The experience obtained by combining humanistic and scientific courses and the exposure to the exciting new methods of learning introduced by the various visiting teachers gave Bernard the initial stimuli to start experimenting with his own creativity. At the age of sixteen he wrote his first narrative *La giornata del giovane Ulisse* (The Day of Young Ulysses; 1971). The Roman publisher Gremese published this semi-autobio-

THE PIT

Enrico Bernard

graphical short story in a new series labeled "Nuove Scritture", distributed free, locally by the Gremese bookstore. Authors and close friends like Vasco Pratolini and Domenico Rea were so impressed with the fifteen page story that parodied the structure of James Joyce's masterpiece that they began a regular literary correspondence with the young writer. This was followed by a series of meetings in Pratolini's house that reinforced an even closer friendship between the two and at the same time gave the young Bernard the needed confidence to continue writing. This unexpected early success convinced him to write a second short story, *Voce del verbo io* (Conjugating the Verb 1), well liked by Giacinto Spagnoletti, but that the author chose not to publish for personal reasons. By the early Eighties the strong conflict within himself (possibly feeling in competition with his father's work) was such that Enrico Bernard stopped writing narrative fiction.

Bernard's strong interest in the arts extended beyond literature and soon he was pursuing his musical interests. The many lessons in classical and modern guitar that he had taken in his teens were helpful first in putting together a short-lived rock group and then in following a more professional career as a singer and song-writer that saw him perform in Roman locales including the popular Folkstudio Theatre where he made his debut in 1974. The serious efforts spent on his musical cabaret compositions would prove to be a great asset later on for his theater. One of his compositions was liked so much by Cesare Zavattini that the poet and movie director included Bernard's song *La verità* (The Truth) in his film script *La verità* (1983). Also, the poet Filippo Accrocca published some of Bernard's compositions in local journals and music magazines

that he was editing at the time.

Between 1976 and 1980, at the University of Rome, Bernard studied linguistics, German literature and philosophy. During this period of formal education he enjoyed combining his literary and musical vocation with his growing love for German philosophers and playwrights. In 1979, during the preparation of his doctoral thesis on the socio-historical and linguistic analysis of terrorism in Germany, Bernard was working on the cultural page of the Roman daily newspaper "Paese Sera" and on interviews with personalities from the entertainment world. The thesis was completed in 1980; it received the highest grades and was published in 1986 with the title *Ideologia piccolo borghese e violenza politica* (Petit Bourgeois Ideology and Political Violence). For the next four years he worked for the publishing house Editori Riuniti and translated the works of Ludwig Tieck and von Chamisso. It was especially his translation of Tieck's *Il mondo alla rovescia* (The World Upside Down), from which he derived a radio show, that made a strong impact on Bernard's future work. From Tieck he had learned to consider the theater «as an instrument to undermine and upset both the real and the unreal while being a vehicle for a deeper social awareness of the subject matter performed.»

In 1979 Bernard completed his first play *Mille e non più mille* (One Thousand and No Longer a Thousand) which was published in 1981 and first staged in 1984. The play is a most original adaptation of Part Two of Goethe's *Faust* In the text the author has mixed dialogues with contemporary punk rock music. Critics such as Ruggiero Jacobbi, Luciano Lucignani and Franco Cordelli were among the reviewers who appreciated Bernard's experiment and their positive reaction

Rocco Capozzi

served as encouragement for the young playwright to keep writing original and stimulating plays.

In 1984 the author began collaborating with the Roman stage director and producer Giuseppe Rossi Montesano who within a decade staged several of his plays such as *Autori! Si nasce* (Authors! One Is Born an Author), *Da cosa nasce cosa* (One Thing Leads to Another), and *Aspettando il '68* (Waiting for 1968).

Throughout the Eighties, while he was intensifying his activities of writing and producing theatrical pieces Bernard was also undertaking the role of editor. The editorial skills that he had learned working for the state owned radio and TV network (known as RAI) publishing house were put to use when he began his own small but prestigious publishing house E&A dedicated primarily to Italian theater. In nearly twenty years he published over 120 volumes. Among these volumes appear the complete theatrical works of Aldo Nicolj and one of his major editorial enterprises, the *Enciclopedia degli autori italiani di teatro 1945-1988* (The Theatre Encyclopedia of Italian Authors 1945-1988) which saw two updated editions in 1990 and 1992.

During the second half of the Eighties Bernard also began to express his passion for film making. The close relationship with actors (from both theater and cinema), directors and producers that he had established through his connections during the period when he worked at the Roman office of RAI helped him get his first job as a consultant on a major movie, *Il volo* (The Flight), directed by Theo Angheloupulos and starring Marcello Mastroianni. In 1985 he also worked with Giuliano Montaldo and Maria Bellonci on the production of the TV movie *Marco Polo*. In the midst of his

film making activities he was also conducting an in depth research on the theme of Faust in German literature. In 1986 the author wrote a script for the staging of his father's first novel, *Tre operai* (Three Workers). The play was staged in Rome and in Cotrone, two of the cities where the action of the novel takes place.

In 1987 Bernard staged *Da cosa nasce cosa*, a one act play, whose main character, Scacciapensieri (literally: 'thoughts chaser'), is a puppet that wishes to be a person. The other characters, unlike the puppet, have no names, they are simply: a man, 'Lui', his wife, 'Lei', and their neighbor, 'un altro'. The play begins as we see a neighbor trying to plug his ears in order not to hear the loud arguments and insults shouted by the couple next door. The set is a typical bourgeois interior. In some quick flashback scenes we see the wife talking with her childhood puppet named Scacciapensieri. But it is not very long before the same puppet comes to life and little by little manages to take over the entire play.

Scacciapensieri, a clear emanation of the wife's childhood games and memories, is also a symbol of her disillusionment, frustration and unfulfilled desires. Once the puppet affirms his new (live) role in her life he becomes impossible to get rid of as he interjects his own comments in every conversation to the point that wife, husband and neighbor begin to fight among themselves. Short and sharp dialogues keep the fast-moving action on stage lively and entertaining throughout the entire act. The play may indeed be a comedy but humor becomes bitter satire once we notice how the characters begin to behave like puppets and that it is the marionette who is really in charge. Scacciapensieri turns from confident to master and in short what was once a security blanket for the wife

Enrico Bernard

gradually becomes a nightmare. By the end of the play it also becomes obvious that the puppet is the only one who is truly rational and who behaves like a real human being. The three characters, on the other hand, feeling defeated in their attempts to get rid of the puppet, resort to feigning their own deaths hoping that he will finally go away, and in so doing behave like marionettes.

Strong shades of Ludwig Tieck, Tommaso Marinetti and Luigi Pirandello are clearly in the background of the play (most certainly in the idea of furniture and marionettes that speak and come to life) but this is not what gives strength to the performance. It is Bernard's familiar witty and ironic language that makes the play an intelligent criticism of empty individuals, caught in a cliché bourgeois love triangle, and who become, much too easily, toys in the hands of a puppet.

In 1989 the author gave to the director Borghesani his text *Autori? Si nasce!* confident that his new farce about neighbors would please audiences and critics. The main characters of this fast moving hilarious comedy are a condominium manager who turns out to be a frustrated and opportunistic comedy writer, a tenant who is a paranoid choreographer, and four other tenants with their own personal problems and agenda. The author here plays with the question: can a condominium board meeting become the subject of a theatrical play? The answer is yes, if in fact the audience appreciates that the play is nothing more than the story/script being written under their eyes; that is, the play is derived from the nonsense that takes place at the meeting and in the building, and is being acted on stage.

The curtain opens as the meeting is about to start with some difficulties. There are not enough members pres-

ent for a quorum and those who are attending keep entering and exiting the room. In the second act one of the tenants asks the manager to come up to his apartment to inspect, supposedly, some problems with the appliances. Things suddenly get complicated. Doors open and close as the gentleman's wife (a striking Spanish lady) and her lover appear and disappear rapidly in the living room, bathroom and kitchen as they try to hide. The confusion and fighting that had started in the meeting room now continues in the upstairs apartment. The administrator is recording everything and his notes will become the material for the theatrical performance. It is in fact the tenants themselves who provide the setting, the dialogues and the intrigues for the manager's script. And thus, as the play unfolds we see the manager become writer, playwright and even psychoanalyst in the process of taking notes and handling the unruly tenants and the secret lovers.

In typical Bernard fashion the dialogues in *Autori si nasce* are a mixture of colloquialisms, everyday language, *non sequiturs*, and absurd statements. The manager's notes/text becomes a metaphor for the author's play being staged. Bernard uses meta-theatrical strategies often enough that his audience can readily accept the notion of the theater within the theater as background material. In the foreground, on the other hand, spectators can appreciate the vivid dialogues between characters who, once again, utter words and expressions that do not seem to have any effect in communicating ideas or feelings. Consequently, the building that is falling apart will continue to go unattended because the tenants and the manager are too busy with their own problems and personal interests. As mentioned, the title of the play is revealed to be an ironic allusion

Rocco Capozzi

to the fact that the author, the characters and the script were being created in front of the audience's eyes. The play is in fact a comical representation of the theatricality of daily life, but the humor does not prevent the audience from leaving the theater laughing at the ridiculous behavior of the tenants and at the same time thinking of themselves as tenants in an equally crazy ambience: our contemporary society.

In 1990 Bernard wrote the *Manifesto S-Naturalismo* (Manifesto S-Naturalism) that the journal of contemporary theater "Ridotto" published in 1993 with illustrations by Dario Fo. The Manifesto, in addition to being a synthesis of Bernard's experiences with his own theater, from the late seventies to the late eighties, is also a reaction to Neo-realistic trends still popular in cinema and theater in Italy. The Manifesto advocates innovations in the fields of art and theater in an age that relied more and more on the mechanical reproduction of art and when everyday language was so highly influenced by the media and in particular by TV that meaningful communication has become more and more difficult. Although in his manifesto Bernard made no mention of Walter Benjamin's well-known essay *The work of art in the age of mechanical reproduction* (1936), it is clear that Bernard was inspired by the German theorist from the School of Frankfurt (that also included Herbert Marcuse and Theodore W. Adorno). Drawing his notions on familiar themes and elements especially from Bertold Brecht, Italian Futurism and the French Theatre of the Absurd, Bernard was advocating that the theater should assume a revolutionary function – not in a political sense – but as a dialectical art form that constantly renews itself. The Manifesto drew the attention of Dario

Fo who later placed it on his website.

In the early Nineties a series of incidents changed Bernard's life and artistic interests. First of all he was deeply saddened by the death of his father in 1992, and, two years later, of his mother Marcella. He had been very close to his parents and had looked after them and their daily needs especially during their illnesses. He was also disturbed by the frequency of mafia and political terrorist crimes that in the late Seventies saw the deaths of several high profile judges and political figures in Italy. These are two key factors responsible for the author's choice to leave Italy and move to Switzerland where he became a citizen. Meanwhile he continued to enjoy success in Rome with his theatrical productions.

In 1991 Bernard saw one of his most political plays, *Aspettando il '68* receive plenty of attention as critics referred to Becket's *Waiting for Godot* for some of their analogies. The allusions in the title are in fact to the 1968 student demonstrations that took place all over Europe and the U.S.A; they may not be as explicit today as they still were a decade ago when people often referred to the historical events of 1968-69. The '68 revolution gave a new awareness to both students and workers from around the world about the covert actions and motives of the 'establishment' (a popular term in the Sixties used to refer to the powerful structures of governments and big business) that controlled everything and everyone.

Like Becket's characters who wait endlessly in *Waiting for Godot*, Bernard's four characters wait at a bus stop for a bus that will never come. On a sidewalk, in a non-descriptive area of Rome, are waiting a middle-aged local woman with a supermarket shopping cart (she never stops talking and frequently uses expressions from TV and

Enrico Bernard

newspaper commercials), a distinguished looking gentleman, an American lady tourist, and a Tunisian illegal immigrant street vendor who is trying to sell everything from rugs, to sunglasses, flashlights and a whole paraphernalia of cheap objects that nobody seems to want. In the midst of the loud chattering of the lady and the high pitched selling of the vendor, a young thief arrives at the scene and robs both the American lady and the gentleman. Within seconds the thief runs away but not before making the gentleman drop his trousers. As the one-act play comes to a close the audience sees the chatty lady pick up the bus stop sign and carry it away looking for a new location where the robbery/play can resume all over again with new victims. By now it becomes evident that the young thief is the lady's son. Furthermore, just before the curtain closes we hear the same words that the lady had spoken in opening line of the play. These words now make more sense. She had said: «In the beginning there was the Word, but what was it? to be or to have?»(in Italian there is a play on words as the biblical expression is literally In the beginning was the Verb).

Aspettando il '68 is certainly entertaining but it is also a highly political play, historically relevant and ideologically grounded in an era that expands from the late Sixties to the late nineties. The Nineties had seen Rome and the rest of Italy attract numerous immigrants from outside the European common market (the so called *extracomunitari*, people from countries other than those members of the European Union).

The Tunisian vendor who arrives on the stage from the center aisle, among the audience, is a symbol of those 'who have not' and who see Italy as the land of hope. The tourist and the gentleman are obviously among those who "have" and who become the target for those who do not have much.

Staged in 1992, *Display* is about two bourgeois couples that at first seem to know each other and then act as if they were complete strangers. The opening scene gives the impression that we are about to witness a wife swapping encounter rather than a séance. The couple is indeed about to stage a *séance* hoping to awaken a spirit that will give them the winning lottery numbers. A spirit does come out but he is speaking in gibberish, a language that no one understands, mainly because he seems to be discussing difficult philosophical concepts about life. In terms of the staging of the play, it must be noted that the action taking place on stage is meant to appear as if it were coming from a TV set and is part of a TV sitcom.

The English title *Display* is meant to refer specifically to a monitor or more specifically to a TV screen. The stage is in fact constructed to resemble a giant screen. However, the term 'display' also alludes to the type of performance taking place both in front of the audience and in the theater itself among the seats and in the aisles. And what could be seen as the opening scene of a situation comedy soon proves to be a farcical, insane, chaotic, and nonsensical encounter of four characters who before the play ends will join the audience, and thus, symbolically, join a collective madness.

Display succeeds very well in depicting Bernard's criticism of a so-called technological society completely conditioned to the point that rather than speaking is spoken by a language derived from (and invented) by the media. The stage within the stage is like the proverbial Chinese box; the whole notion of the theater within the theater is further reinforced by the actors's action of interacting with the

Rocco Capozzi

spectators. Once the two couples come down from the stage and begin to mingle with the audience a loud noise is heard while powerful blinding strobe lights invade the entire theater. Havoc takes over until a sign appears on stage: «Silence. A play is on». As the curtain comes down the audience hears the same words that had opened the play: «The theater must only entertain... there is always time to die».

Prigioniero della sua proprietà (Prisoner of His Own Property) was staged in 1992. The play is one of Bernard's most original and fascinating experimental plays which is also full with surprises. From the very beginning the spectators know that they are not to witness a traditional play. As they enter the theater they are told by the announcer that one comes in free and goes out paying for the performance. Moreover the play begins with the Epilogo and closes with the Prologo. The music that is heard periodically throughout the two acts has been composed entirely by the author.

The two-act play is centered around the question, what would happen if a man one day woke up and realized that he has become two different people? The main protagonist, 'Il Signor Uno Qualsiasi' (Mister Common Man) is, in fact, two opposite characters in one. On one side he is a victim of robberies and on the other he is the thief who robs himself.

Uno Qualsiasi is basically an instrument with which the author and audience examine what is happening to social and community values and also how irrational people have become in trying to beat the so-called social system that they no longer trust.

The story becomes more intriguing once the protagonist starts demanding that police, investigators, government officials, and his lawyer look after his concerns. It is fascinating to see Uno Qualsiasi train guard dogs and buy complex electronic security systems while at the same time continuing to rob from his own home. Bernard, who is a master at using different language registers, here combines the colloquial with the bureaucratic, as well as the legalese with the philosophical, as we hear the language of lawyers, secretaries, investigators, and police, all trying to deal with the man's problems.

The play takes a surprising turn when Uno Qualsiasi is asked to prove his existence by providing birth certificates and testimonials. At this point echoes of Luigi Pirandello abound and these intertextual allusions remain throughout the second and third acts. The play closes as the man, in a straight jacket and staring into the void, is about to be taken to an insane asylum. It is interesting to note that the main protagonist, even with his unending obvious farcical contradictions never becomes a caricature of himself. Rather, his state of alienation and his words and actions make the audience think, and rightly so, that perhaps it is society that has become alienating and in many ways it has become a caricature of itself, or a big joke.

In the Fall of 1992 Enrico Bernard was recognized as an outstanding playwright when he received two important prizes: first, the Premio Istituto del Dramma Italiano (for is drama *Magnetic Theater Play*) and, soon after, the prestigious Maschera D'Argento, for his overall work in the theater.

In 1995, when Bernard first staged *Un mostro di nome Lila,* he would have never guessed that his new play would become of his most talked about work. Eros and Thanatos, the erotic and the nightmarish, Faust and Freud, are all perfectly (con)fused in this extremely intense drama that Italian and German reviewers defined as an erotic psychological thriller. This one act play is per-

THE PIT

Enrico Bernard

haps a rare instance when Bernard chooses to focus not on socio-political issues and on the mechanisms and strategies of the theater of his favorite playwrights that he so often recalls, but rather on the private and hidden sector of the human psyche. It is also a play that allows the author to play with Freudian symbols and double meanings.

The setting for the story is an empty restaurant room somewhere in a wooded area of a Nordic region. The characters are a girl and a man. The play begins as it is still dark, early in the morning. Empty tables await the arrival of patrons. A beautiful and provocative waitress moves nervously around the room. Suddenly a stranger arrives, dressed in black, claiming that his car has broken down.

In a matter of minutes begins a dramatic duet between the man (the monster?) and the girl (a victim?) as they begin to battle with a series of questions and accusations. The whole dialogue is about bringing to the surface not so much her memories but Lila's hidden feelings, fears, anxieties, animalistic instinct, sexuality, and intimate fantasies. The restaurant room soon becomes a psychoanalytical and oneiric playground. The dialogues, as well as the familiar symbols such as a stranger dressed in black, and a young woman alone in an isolated house in the woods, provide the material and images for a suspenseful erotic mystery. In the verbal exchanges (at times accompanied by brief erotic bodily contacts) between Lila and the stranger the audience witnesses how the invented images of a bad dream, or better, of an incubus, becomes a reality. During the entire heated argument Lila, although fighting back and at times blaming the stranger for her troubles, turns out to be making an actual confession of her deep feelings of guilt and past sins.

In the closing scene the mystery surrounding Lila is somewhat resolved as the first rays of sunlight appear through the fixtures. It becomes clear that the duel was a manifestation of the struggle between Lila's subconscious and her external facade put on for herself and for others. From the dialogues we learn that Lila has grown up seeking in and through her sexuality the warmth of human affection. But now her alter ego has decided to rebel. Doctor Jekyll and Mr. Hyde, light and darkness, love and sex have resorted to battling one another. It is not clear which side of Lila will win.

Un mostro di nome Lila is Bernard's most powerful play that focuses specifically on feelings, emotions and psychological issues related to guilt. It is also the play that has won the most approval of both the audience and critics wherever it has been staged. By the same token with *Un mostro di nome Lila* some critics will speak of Bernard's interest in treating light eroticism on stage. In fact, and on a much lighter level, the only other play in which one could possibly speak of sexual innuendos and light eroticism is *La commedia dell'usignolo* (The Nightingale's Comedy). Here two couples leave the city for the countryside where they can experience a new and uninhibited sexual freedom. However, by the end of the play it becomes obvious that for the couple, the plan to materialize their erotic fantasies fails.

Bernard's interests in filmmaking were materialized in the late nineties. In 1997, during one of his frequent returns from Switzerland, to Rome and to the world of theater, he met, through his acquaintance with film director Tinto Brass, the Hungarian adult entertainment star, Eva Henger, who had been made popular by Italian TV and newspapers. She agreed to

Rocco Capozzi

play the central role in the film adaptation of *Un mostro di nome Lila* and to appear in another film under his direction. Bernard was well aware that he was capitalizing on the popularity of Eva Henger; however he did this primarily in order to focus on the cultural transgressions that he was portraying in his theater and films in the late Nineties.

There is no doubt that one of the most prevailing issues for Bernard's characters is the problem with communication, or better the lack of, in today's society. *La voragine* (The Abyss) is a play that several critics like Paolo Petroni, Aggeo Savioli, Giorgio Serafini and Pietro Favari have raved about in their reviews especially for the way the author uses language and dialogues reminiscent of the French Theatre of the Absurd. *La voragine* illustrates how skillful Bernard can be when he employs very few characters and decides to focus primarily on the verbal exchanges between them. This is indeed the case between Ori, the worker, and his foreman, Il capo, the two characters who throughout the two acts discuss back and forth a variety of topics ranging from the useless vortex that has been excavated for no particular reason, to the relationships between employers and workers, and to the impossibility of understanding one another simply because, even though they speak the same language and use the same words in reality they do not communicate since words have different meanings for them. In essence one speaks from the point of view of a worker and one from that of a person in charge and with power.

At the end of 1999 Bernard moved back to Rome. After having written and staged twelve theatrical works he arrived at the difficult decision that perhaps it was time to concentrate almost exclusively on the art of film-making. Immediately after the completion, in Switzerland, of the *Il gioco dei sensi* (The Senses Game), in October of 2002, he began plans to shoot a script adapted from his father's well known novel *Il giorno degli assassinii* (The Day of Assassinations, 1980) that focuses on political terrorism and crime in general.

After seven years of absence from the Roman stages, in May of 2003 Bernard returned to the theater with a new unpublished light-hearted comedy, a one act play: *Cenerentola assassina* (Cinderella, the Assassin). It is a psychological mystery drama centered on the interrogation by the police of an unnamed girl found wondering in the streets of Rome, covered with blood. Is she the victim or the assassin? The indications at the end of the play are that she is indeed both. The play is in part a parody of the 1999 Hollywood film, *The Fight Club*, starring Edward Norton and Brad Pitt. In Bernard's text Cinderella, and other women, once they graduate from the 'female fight club' they go out on the Roman streets looking for a male victim in order to test their skills.

Although the mystery about the unknown girl is not solved in the present one act play, the audience has no difficulty in guessing that Cinderella, who has at least two different names, is far from being only a victim. The longer version will certainly solve this and other questions that now remain open at the end of *Cenerentola assassina*.

In their attempt to label Enrico Bernard's theater under one easy banner critics like Paolo Petroni, Emilia Costantini and Katia Ippaso have conveniently resorted to speaking of the author's predilection for the absurd. This may be true in part if one also points out that in his theater the absurd is always rooted in realism. Nonetheless, it is important to notice

Enrico Bernard

that as Bernard experiments with his theater that focuses mainly on the absurd, the irrational and the nonsense, that prevails in our society, he is not afraid of being accused of imitating the great masters of modern theater such as Pirandello, Becket, Ionesco, or Campanile.

In Enrico Bernard's original and stimulating plays there are certain elements that have become his trademarks. For one thing spectators notice very few actors on stage and the use of a language that is best characterized by quick lively and colorful dialogues. In the witty verbal exchanges the audience can appreciate the humorous popular colloquialisms as well as the ironic and thought provoking statements directed not only at the situations being represented but also at the language used by the characters. Other familiar features of Bernard's theater are the exploitations of empty white walls, unexpected flooding of white lights that hit the stage from different angles, loud noises, and the interjection of original music that the author himself has composed. Furthermore, underneath his entertaining representations one can always find profound philosophical undertones linked to the universal themes of loss of freedom, difficulties in communicating, and alienation in a hyper-consumerist society which plague the human spirit.

In October of 2003 Bernard reprinted his *Manifesto del teatro S-Naturalista* in the first volume of his collected plays: *Teatro S-Naturalista.* In addition to twelve of his texts which follow the manifesto, the volume includes an appendix where the author has reprinted several reviews of his plays by leading critics such as Renzo Tian, Franco Cordelli, Pietro Favari, Emilia Costantini, and Giorgio Prosperi who have followed his work for the last two decades.

Bernard's plays have been widely appreciated by spectators and critics especially for the way the author mixes ironic and parodic language with phrases and words that are clear echoes of his favorite German, French and Italian playwrights. Ludwig Tieck, Franz Kafka, Hans Von Kleist, Eugene Ionesco, Samuel Becket, Tommaso Marinetti, Luigi Pirandello, Rosso di San Secondo, and Achille Campanile. In his plays the author wishes to take the spectators beyond the level of entertainment hoping that they will also ponder on today's loss of identity, individuality, naturalness, and traditional values, in a society that has fallen into the traps of mediocrity and superficiality, as a result of the overwhelming conditioning effects of TV and, to put it succinctly, the postmodern mishmash of mass media in general.

Bernard's theater is consistently a combination of the provocative and the playful as it combines with great ease, ironic, parodic, philosophical, irreverent, and sarcastic elements directed not just towards the characters and situations represented on stage but also towards the very same theater (from the days of Futurism to the experimental theater of the 70s), that he echoes in his work. Sharp humor, quick dialogues, and plenty of special effects of sounds and lights are key elements of Bernard's theater that spectators have learned to expect from his comedies and dramas. Also, in Bernard's plays often characters are depersonalized and do not have names. This is in essence part of the author's strategy to universalize as much as possible the messages being delivered by his characters. Furthermore, even though the ideological underlining of Bernard's theater is not always visible because the plays may seem lighthearted and parodic, the author can be nonetheless extremely mordant in his criticism of a contemporary society that appears to be drowning in superficial conventionalities.

SELECTED WORKS BY ENRICO BERNARD

La spiaggia equestra (clowneria), Rome, Veberi, 1979.

La commedia degli e/orrori, Rome, Veberi, 1979.

Su e giù dal gran mondo borghese di Faust, Rome, Veberi, 1980.

Mehr Licht. Quante storie per un cantastorie, Rome, Veberi, 1980.

Mille e non più mille. Edited by Luciano Lucignani, Rome, Veberi, 1981.

"Anche la morte ha un cuore", *Theatron*, XXIII, 289, May-August 1983: 55-60.

"Prigioniero della sua proprietà", *Ridotto*, 1-3, January-March 1985: 72-103.

Ideologia piccolo borghese e violenza politica, Rome, E&A, 1986.

"Manifesto del teatro S-Naturalista", *Ridotto*, 1-2, January/February 1993: 44-53.

"Un mostro di nome Lila", *Ridotto*, 45, December 1996: 14-29; *Ein Ungeheyuer Namens Lila*, translated by S. Heymann, *TheaterHeute*, Wuppenau, Verleger gmbh, 1994; *A Monster Named Lila and Prisoner of His Property*, translated by Toni De Graff, Rocco Capozzi and Celestino De Juliis, Toronto, Scholars Press, 2006.

Teatro S-Naturalista, Rome, E&A, 2003.

La voragine, Rome, E&A, 2003; *Die Grube*, German translation of *La voragine*, *Buch zum Theater*, 3, 1997: 6-11.

Prisoner of His Own Property-A Monster Called Lila, Toronto, Soleil, 2006.

La voragine, Edizioni Studio 12, Rome, 2008.

"Tre Operai", *Ridotto*, 1-2, January/February 2011.

Teatro della crisi del capitalismo; Comprises *Prigioniero della sua proprietà, Tre operai, Holy Money, Taken to the Cleaner, Big Bang*, Rome, Entertainmentart, 2011.

"Holy Money" (in Italian, English, Franch and German), *Rivista di Studi Italiani*, XXXI, 1, 2012: 335-383.

Holy Money, Rome, Bulzoni, 2013.

"Assolo contro la a'ndrangheta" in *Assoli contro la mafia Trogen*, Be@Teatro, 2013.

SELECTED PREMIERES

Ballate teatrali, Rome, Folkstudio, 22 October 1974.

Mille e non più mille, Rome, Teatro La Scaletta, 9 February 1984.

Il Pentapentito, *Rome, Teatro La Scaletta, 12 November 1985.*

La classe operaia non va in paradiso; first adaptation of C. Bernari's novel *Tre operai*, Rome, Teatro Alla Ringhiera, 15 February 1986.

Da cosa nasce cosa, Rome, Teatro Tordinona, 14 October 1987.

Autori? si nasce!, Rome, Teatro Argot, 2 May 1989.

I creativi, Rome, Teatro Argot, 5 May 1990.

Aspettando il 68, Rome, Teatro dell'Orologio, 23 May 1991.

Prigioniero della sua proprietà, Rome, Teatro Politecnico, 6 January 1992.

Magnetic Theater Play, Rome, Teatro Tordinona, 17 April 1992.

Display. Rome, Teatro Tordinona, 23 November 1992.

La commedia dell'usignolo, Rome, Teatro Centrale, 3 May 1994.

Un mostro di nome Lila, Rome, Teatro Politecnico, 9 May 1995.

La voragine, Rome, Teatro Politecnico,

3 March 1997.
Cenerentola assassina, Rome, Teatro Belli, 3 May 2003.
Mary Shelley e Frankenstein, Rome Teatro Tordinona, 15 March 2005.
Tre operai, Rome, Teatro Ateneo, 23 May 2005.

SELECTED BIBLIOGRAPHY

Boggio, M. "Dal teatro nasce altro teatro", *Avanti*, 14 October 1987: 11.

Boggio, M. "Il palazzo crolla, rissa tra condomini", *Avanti*, 22 April 1989: 11.

Capozzi, R. "Interview with Enrico Bernard", *Rivista di studi italiani*, XX, Spring 2004: 147-155.

Chiaretti, T. "Faust vittima del denaro. Mille e non più mille", *La Repubblica*. 4 February, 1984.

Cordelli, F. "Diavolaccio d'un Mephisto che coltiva utopie", *Paese Sera*, 14 February 1984: 16.

Cordelli, F. "Giochiamo all'amore con una marionetta. Da cosa nasce cosa", *Paese Sera*, 11 October 1987: 17.

Costantini, E. "Autori si nasce", *Corriere della sera*, 4 May 1989: 25.

Costantini, E. "L'eros e la fanciulla, una notte inconfessabile. Un mostro di nome Lila", *Corriere della sera*, 11 May, 1985: 25.

Costantini, E. "I creativi", *Corriere della sera*, 11 May, 1990: 25.

Costantini, E. "Un furto esemplare", *Corriere della sera*, 27 January 1992: 26.

Costantini, E. "Un'odissea degli insetti", *Corriere della sera*, 13 April 1992: 26.

Costantini, E. "L'eros e la fanciulla", *Corriere della sera*, 11 May 1995: 25.

Costantini, E. "Debutto di Eva Henger con il Dottor Freud", *Corriere della sera*, 7 October 1998: 27.

De Chiara, G. "Una favola nera con sovrani da operetta", *Avanti*, 7 February 1984: 12.

Di Giammarco, R. "Tre operai", *La Repubblica*, 18 February 1986: 19.

Di Giammarco, R. "Da cosa nasce cosa", *La Repubblica*, 29 October 1987: 19.

Di Giammarco, R. "L'autobus non arriva in via dell'assurdo", *Corriere della sera*, 24 May 1991: 25.

Di Giammarco, R. "Autori! Non si nasce", *La Repubblica*, 26 April 1989: 20.

Favari, P. "Tre operai. La classe operaia non va in paradiso", *Corriere della sera*, 24 February 1986: 26.

Favari, P. "Da cosa nasce cosa", *Corriere della sera*, 15 October 1987: 25.

Favari, P. "Due coppie di amanti al picnic con le ombre", *Corriere della sera*, 7 May 1994: 26.

Favari, P. "La voragine. il capo e il suo operaio", *Corriere della sera*, 11 March 1997: 26.

Garrone, N. "Prigioniero della sua proprietà", *La Repubblica*, 11 January 1992: 19.

Garrone, N. "Bernard: Mary Shelley e Frankenstein", *La Repubblica*, 25 March 2005.

Ippasio, Katia. "Prigioniero della sua proprietà: da Becket si arriva a Ionesco", *Il Tempo*, 7 January 1992: 14.

Prosperi, G. "Tutti in corsa verso il nulla. Autori? Si nasce!", *Il Tempo*, 25 April 1989: 15.

Prosperi, G. "La voragine", *Il Tempo*, 27 March 1997: 15.

Romeo, L. "Questa marionetta è proprio liberty. Da cosa nasce cosa", *Il Tempo*, 13 October 1987: 15.

Roblony, S. "Eva Henger. fantasie erotiche con la luna e richiami a Freud", *La Stampa*, 16 December 1998: 19.

Savioli, A. "Mille e non più mille", *L'U-*

nità, 11 February 1984: 11.

Savioli, A. "Tre operai. La classe operaia non va in paradiso", *L'Unità*, 22 February 1986: 11.

Savioli, A. "Due attori sospesi sull'orlo della voragine", *L'Unità*, 19 March 1997: 12.

Serafini, G. "Enrico Bernard e il teatro della Beffa. Magnetic theater play", *Il Tempo*, 15 April 1992: 16.

Serafini, G. "Display", *Il Tempo*, 17 November 1992: 16.

Serafini, G. "Un mostro di nome Lila", *Il Tempo*, 9 May 1995: 15.

Serafini, G. "Vivere nella voragine", *Il Tempo*, 27 March 1997: 16.

Tian, R. "Da cosa nasce cosa", *Il Messaggero*, 14 October 1987: 21.

Tian, R. "Autori? Si nasce!", *Il Messaggero*, 24 April 1989: 20.

Tian, R. "Display", *Il Messaggero*, 1 December 1992: 22.

Salvai, M. D. "La duplice identità di un uomo qualsiasi", *Momento Sera*, 13 January 1992: 13.

Sansalone, C. "*La voragine e Il Teatro S-Naturalista*", *Rivista di studi italiani*, XX, Spring 2004: 156-161.

Vellella, B. "Il thriller psicologico: Un mostro di nome Lila", *Momento Sera*, 6 May 1995: 13.

ENRICO BERNARD

HYSTRYO
WHILE IN ROME IT SNOWED
A TALE

TRANSLATION BY
MARCO REMO ZANELLI

Enrico Bernard
SAVE·THE·WORLD·KILL·A·CAPITALIST
PACE
HOLY
MONEY
"The last capitalist we hang
shall be the one who sold us
the rope" \ BeaT

Enrico Bernard
EIGHT HATEFUL PLAYS
VIOLENCE
SEXISM
EXCLUSION
FEAR
BeaT

Enrico Bernard
Prisoner of His Own Property
Translated by
Rocco Capozzi
A Monster Called Lila
Translated by
Celestino De Iuliis
SOLEIL